I0731758

MIDNIGHT HEAT

TAMSIN LEY

with

AURORA SHIFTERS

A Production of
Twin Leaf
Press

Paperback version
ISBN-13: 978-1-950027-25-5

The sound of fiddling pierced the cold November air as Captain Elias Sobol hesitated outside the bar's heavy wooden door. The flickering neon sign in the bar's window was making his head swim, and the air had a crackly feel that told him a storm was coming. Even his inner seal was jittery, vibrating with anticipation like that moment right before he plunged into the ocean. *It's just being in a new town.* He didn't like encroaching on another selkie clan's territory. But the entire crew of the *Utkin* was gathering to support Bobby's first band gig, and Elias didn't want to let him down.

His first mate, Jacob, pushed open the door from inside. "You coming? We've got seats up front."

"Yeah, be right there." Elias adjusted his pelt—to humans it appeared as a duster-length sealskin vest—

and stepped inside. Warmth hit his face, carrying with it the overwhelming scent of humanity and spilled beer. Despite it being past the season for tourists, the bar was packed with people, faces lit by strings of Christmas lights criss-crossing the ceiling. Elias immediately spotted Walton's sealskin hat at the front near the low platform where Bobby and his band stood belting out a fast-paced tune.

Turning, he slid sideways through the crowd, weaving between bodies like swimming through long fronds of kelp. Maybe after the band finished playing, he'd go to the beach and shift. Letting his seal out to swim would help clear his mind. As he approached the long bar, a delicious scent reached him—cinnamon and mocha with an underlying hint of what he could only describe as sex.

His heartbeat kicked up, and a single thought consumed him. *Mate.* His eyes came to rest on a short figure with brown curly hair sticking out beneath a pink winter cap. She sat on a bar stool with her back to him, but he could see her delicious womanly curves filling out the sweatshirt and jeans she wore. A true Alaska girl. He couldn't hold back his seal's low growl of approval.

She swiveled in the chair to glance at the band, revealing her profile. Her cheeks were flushed as if she'd just come in out of the cold, and her broad smile shot straight through Elias's heart. The smile wasn't directed at him, however. She was talking to a weathered man with shaggy, dirty-blonde surfer hair sitting beside to her.

Elias rolled his shoulders, shaking off the possessive aggression settling over him. Not all shifters found their true mates, but when they did, the physical attraction was supposed to be instantaneous and undeniable. He only hoped they had human things in common, as well.

He silently chided his inner seal, *You knew she was here all along, didn't you?*

His seal responded by filling his mind with lusty thoughts.

Feeling his body respond in embarrassing ways, he shook his head but couldn't help the smile tugging his lips. They said meeting one's mate for the first time was something you'd never forget. *I'd prefer she didn't remember our first meeting as me being a perv who approached her at the bar.* Elias straightened his shoulders, pulled his vest closed over his front, and nudged past a group standing between him and the woman.

His mate didn't appear to have sensed him yet, and as he drew near, he understood why; her cinnamon scent grew stronger, but it also told him she was human.

Damn. That put a kink in things. Humans weren't as in-tune with their instincts—he was going to have to woo her now and find a way to reveal his true nature later. He paused a few bar stools away, taking a moment to plan his new strategy. On stage, Bobby was playing his heart out on the fiddle, the guitarist strumming an accompanying beat while the vocalist shouted something about gambling away his heart.

Elias's future mate bobbed her head in time to the music.

I could ask her to dance.

His seal laughed at him, knowing full well Elias didn't dance.

Someone at a table near him reached out to tug his sleeve. "Hey, Elias," a woman shouted above the music. "What are you doing in Kenai? Buy me a drink?"

He pulled back and it took him a second to recognize her. He'd met her in Homer last year, and they'd spent a few enjoyable nights together, but hell if he could remember her name. He forced himself to smile but shook his head. "Not tonight, love."

The woman stuck out her lip in a pout, but he moved past without another glance. At least she'd had the right idea. *Start by offering to buy a drink.*

He was within arms length of his mate when he spotted the metallic glint on her left hand. *Married?*

He glanced once more at the man next to her. She was totally out of that guy's league. Was the ring a ploy to keep guys from hitting on her? He'd met women who did that. He started forward again. Suddenly, the man next to her grabbed her chin in one hand and kissed her. Not a peck, but a deep, satisfying, intimate kiss.

Elias's spine stiffened. Before his brain had time to catch up, he'd grabbed the guy by the back of his collar and yanked him off his stool, tossing him onto the floor.

The crowd surged back, giving the fallen man room.

"What the hell?" the guy shouted, face dark with fury.

"The lady doesn't appreciate being mauled," Elias answered, peripherally aware that the woman had risen to her feet behind him.

The guy sat up, drawing his feet under him to stand. "She's my wife, you asshole."

A lead weight settled to the bottom of Elias's stomach. "Shit."

He turned to find the woman gaping at him, brown eyes wide. Then she turned her lovely face away to look at her husband on the floor. *Husband. Wife.* The ring wasn't an act.

If there was one boundary Elias wouldn't cross, this was it; he wouldn't steal another man's wife.

Something hard slammed into Elias's cheek, rocking his head back. Stumbling, he turned in time to receive a second jab directly in the eye. Stars filled his vision, and his own fists flew up on instinct. The man was back on his feet, fists in front of him like a boxer. He jabbed again. This time, Elias dodged the blow.

Someone in the crowd yelled, "Fight!"

"Peter, stop," the woman shouted, reaching with both hands for her husband's arm.

Elias seldom started brawls—at least, not without good reason. But he also wasn't one to back down from one. Still, the guy had a right to be pissed. Elias forced his fists open and raised both palms in front of him. "I thought she was someone else. Honest mistake."

The man danced forward. "Honest my ass. Come on and fight, you pussy."

The band had stopped playing and the crowd had formed a surging ring around the area. A grizzled bouncer shoved into the open space. "Break it up, Peter." He held out both arms as he stepped between them and glared at Elias. "Both of you, take it outside."

Above the crowd, Elias felt Jacob's eyes on him and the telepathic bond he shared with his selkie crew surged to life. *Need backup?*

What a fiasco. He didn't need his crew knowing he'd found his mate. If they did, they'd do everything they could to break up her marriage, and if they did that, he may as well just steal her away right now. Keeping all thoughts of his mate out of his mind, Elias shook his head and sent back, *Nope. I'm done. Tell Bobby I'm sorry.*

Turning, Elias jetted out the door and into the cold night air, ignoring Peter's drunken taunts as he climbed into his pickup. He was halfway home before he cooled down enough to realize he hadn't even learned his mate's name.

CHAPTER TWO

*L*ana counted out bills and lay them on the counter in front of the marine supply store clerk. Behind her, the small store buzzed with activity. Fish and Wildlife's sonar had reported what they called "a wall of fish" headed up the inlet. Tomorrow was the commercial opening, and everyone was scrambling to get ready. Tomorrow would be her lucky break. She could feel it in her soul.

Running a fishing operation was expensive, but in for a penny, in for a pound, as her husband used to say. Money had been tight since his death a year ago, but she was determined to keep at this fishing thing. If she'd learned anything during their brief marriage, it was that the ocean was in her blood, and she loved nothing more than the salt of the wind on her face and the roll of the waves under her feet.

A deep laugh was followed by a man's angry cursing, and she glanced toward two fishermen arguing one aisle over. Rivalry could get aggressive, and tension was high. Peter had come to blows more than once with a few of the captains, although that had usually been at the bar. She'd even had to bail him out of jail two years ago, not only keeping them off the water for an entire day, but also spending most of their income from the next day's catch.

The clerk handed her a receipt, unperturbed by the nearby argument. "Weatherman's predicting a blowout —you know, a storm? Be careful out there, sweetheart."

She'd heard that, too, and was a little nervous—enough that she didn't let the clerk's mansplaining or his condescending endearment goad her. The salmon run would hit the mouth of the river in less than twenty-four hours, and she had to make the most of the opportunity. Only by some twist of luck had her loan officer pulled enough strings to give her until the end of this season to catch up on her boat payments.

"Thanks, I will." She picked up the heavy replacement prop with both hands. The *Willy Nilly's* current prop worked okay, but the new one would provide a lot more get-up-and-go if she could install it before tomorrow.

She turned toward the exit and collided with sleek silver fur. Her stomach dropped. *Elias Sobol.* The broad chest and sealskin vest gave away his identity as surely as any photo ID. Her late husband might've been a brawling, cheating, son-of-a-bitch, but Elias Sobol was the definition of asshole. And she knew better than to take any shit from a man like him.

She looked up into his nearly black irises and scowled. "Excuse you."

He raised his brows but didn't move. The man wasn't exactly handsome, but he was... interesting. Powerful shoulders, dark shiny hair going silver at the temples, and a raised scar on his forehead bisecting one eyebrow—something she assumed he'd acquired in a bar fight or some other sordid business. His deep voice rumbled, a vibration she could almost feel in her bones. "I recommend sitting this one out, Captain."

He always called her Captain, and she could never tell if he was being derisive or not. She almost preferred he'd call her sweetheart like the rest of the fishing captains. "You're not exactly my go-to for advice, Elias." She shook off the adrenaline-fueled butterflies in her stomach. "Now if you don't mind, I'm in a hurry."

His eyes caught the glow from the florescent bulbs overhead, flashing with power as he wrapped a big hand around her upper arm. "I'm serious, Lana. The *Willy Nilly* isn't made for this weather."

"Don't touch me." She jerked away. "I'll be fine. Now get out of my way. This thing's heavy."

They'd attracted the attention of several onlookers, and a man with a thick brown beard stepped forward.

The man reached for the prop. "Let me help you with that, sweetheart."

Usually insistent on holding her own among the men in the industry, Lana slanted a glance toward Elias and relinquished the part with a broad smile. "That's very kind, thank you."

Elias curled his upper lip and stepped aside. She could feel his gaze on her back as she led the way outside to her beat-up Chevy. The bearded man plunked the prop into the truck bed and brushed his palms against the front of his stained denim jacket. "Hey, I'm having a bonfire this weekend. You should come."

Great, she knew where this was going. Quite a few fishermen had approached her after Peter's death. Even Elias the asshole had tried to hit on her—within a month of Peter's passing, no less. The few she'd elected to date had turned out to be duds. Even so, the last thing she wanted to do was create animosity with yet another fisherman. *Be polite but distant.* She closed the truck's tailgate. "Thanks for the invite, but I've got plans."

"You sure? Bonfire and beer is a better use of your time than trying to fish this storm."

She shook her head. "I'm sure."

"Suit yourself." He shrugged. "Watch yourself out there tomorrow."

"You be careful, too," she said as she climbed into the truck and pulled the door closed.

From the store's doorway, she saw Elias emerge, eyes glued on the bearded man. He was scowling the same way he used to scowl at Peter. What the fuck was wrong with him? She needed to get out of here and worry about her own shit, not whatever competition was going on among everyone else.

She pulled out of the parking lot and headed toward the bakery her parents had owned. Her cousin, Ashlyn, now ran it, but Lana had a tradition of bringing fresh doughnuts to her crew before each launch. She stepped inside, inhaling the wonderful yeasty scent of baking bread. The main thing she missed about the bakery was the smell—heaven compared to the fish-and-diesel scent of her boat.

A couple sat enjoying coffee at the small table near the window, and Ashlyn stood behind the register, her bright pink and blue hair a nice match to the stacks of pink pastry boxes on the shelves behind her. Ashlyn had put on a little weight since she'd moved to Kenai, but not in a bad way. She seemed more muscular, of all things, not rounded from eating too many sweets. "Hey, Lana," she greeted with a smile.

Cal Bennett emerged through the saloon-style swinging doors to the kitchen, his brown State Trooper hat in one hand and a bear claw in the other. "Thanks, Ashlyn," he said, giving Lana a cursory nod as he passed by on his way toward the exit.

The jerk. She'd had a fling with him a while back—if you could call a single night in front of the TV a fling. He was Ashlyn's husband's best friend, but to Lana, he was just one more reason to avoid men.

Ashlyn shook her head and muttered. "I told him he could use the bathroom."

Lana glanced toward the doughnut display case. A woman with three grade school age kids milling about her like satellites blocked it.

As if reading her mind, Ashlyn hooked a thumb over her shoulder. "I saved you three raspberry filled and a few maple bars for Jeanette. Look by the fridge."

Grinning, Lana said, "You're the best."

"You can pay me back in fresh salmon," Ashlyn called after her as Lana pushed into the kitchen.

A pink box on the counter held an assortment of pastries. She pulled a raspberry jelly doughnut out and took a big bite, flooding her mouth with sweet gooey filling. Ashlyn had taken to baking like a boss, and Lana had zero regrets about relinquishing her parents' old business to her cousin. Plus, Lana never charged her for the treats.

Sealing the box with a piece of tape, she headed back out front. "Thanks, Ashlyn. You're the best."

"Wait." Ashlyn handed some change to a woman before turning to Lana and digging into her apron pocket. "You left this on the counter yesterday."

Lana accepted the tiny pocketknife her father had given her the first day she'd gone out on the boat with Peter. The blade was too tiny to be much use, but the worn ivory handle felt good, and she used it as a worry stone. "I wondered where I'd put it. Thanks."

"Can't go without your good luck charm." Ashlyn winked and turned to greet another customer.

Rubbing a thumb over the etched scrimshaw image of a jumping salmon, Lana shoved it into her jeans pocket. She hated to admit it, but she needed all the luck she could get. If she didn't get a handle on this fishing thing, she'd end up right back here working for Ashlyn.

CHAPTER THREE

*R*ain blurred the wheelhouse's windows as Elias piloted the *Utkin* out of the mouth of the river in the wake of the *Willy Nilly*. His seal form preferred to avoid this weather, especially on board a boat; riding what amounted to a big piece of flotsam in these waves could make even a selkie seasick. But he had to protect Lana Gregory—even if she didn't understand why.

After his first encounter with her in the bar almost three years ago, he'd quickly learned she and her husband operated a fishing boat in Kenai. Although he wouldn't steal a man's wife, he still felt all the urges a mate would feel, including the need to be near her and keep her safe. It was biology, pure and simple, but he couldn't fight it, so he'd moved his boat and crew up from Homer the very next season. His men didn't know why, only that he wanted to expand his territory; selkies were notorious for abducting spouses, and he didn't need them offering any "help."

Laughter rose from the cabin below where his crew was guzzling energy drinks and readying themselves for the big push to fill their fish lockers. The *Utkin* was almost twice the size of the *Willy Nilly*, with a crew of four plus the captain—three fellow selkies and the new kid, Dean, a werewolf who swore he was meant to be a "wolf of the sea." Elias had made him pass an excruciating swimming test before taking him on, but the kid succeeded with flying colors, so who was Elias to judge? At least he wasn't human.

Humans were frail, and many didn't respect the ocean like they should. *Including Lana.* But he didn't blame her; she'd learned bad habits from that husband of hers. When Elias had moved to Kenai, he'd assumed it would only be a matter of time before Lana ended the marriage on her own; humans seldom mated for life, and Peter Gregory was wrong for her. Her husband had talked down to her, spent all their money on beer, and had even cheated on her. His saving grace had been that he hadn't laid a hand on her—if there was one thing Elias wouldn't abide, it was a man who beat on women. Elias had bided his time from a distance for all these years, waiting for her to get fed up.

Then Peter had died.

It was one thing to court a woman after a breakup, and quite another to court a widow. The human part of him knew he needed to give her a respectful mourning period, but his seal was fed up with waiting. He managed to hold off approaching her for almost two months before his seal forced the issue when he bumped into her at a fast-food joint, of all places. He'd sputtered out an offer to buy her lunch.

And she'd rebuffed him like he was offering a platter of last-week's discarded fish.

Since then, she'd been even more stand-offish whenever he came near. It seemed that the years of aggressive rivalry between Elias and Peter had solidified Elias Sobol as a villain in Lana's mind.

Turning the *Utkin's* bow into the wind, he pressed on, monitoring the radar blip that indicated the path of the *Willy Nilly*. The woman had a negative sense of direction when it came to fishing, but he had to give her credit for continuing to try. A few times, he'd taken to his seal form to chase the fish into her nets, just to help her out.

Right now, the radar placed her boat awfully near the shallow waters of a rocky shoal—not the place to be fishing in weather like this. Wasn't she paying attention to her charts? The massive waves provided a roller coaster view of the darkening horizon, and any one of them could drive a boat against one of the many submerged rocks in the area. Navigation in the inlet could be tricky, but where the hell was she going?

The *Utkin's* hull smacked against a wave, nearly knocking his feet out from under him, and he was forced to veer slightly off course to keep them from tipping. "Fucking idiot," he grumbled, half at himself, half at Lana. This storm was shaping up to be a doozy.

"Captain?" his first mate said behind him.

Elias glanced over his shoulder to where Jacob stood braced in the doorway, X-tra Tuff boots gripping the deck and sealskin parka dripping water onto the floor. Each selkie wore their pelt differently—Walton wore his as a hat, which looked silly as fuck in the summer, but whatever, and Elias preferred his long duster vest. The magical quality of the pelt could adjust into the shape of any piece of clothing, but more importantly, it gave a selkie the power to shift. Without it, they lost the power to assume their seal form.

Returning his attention to the wheel, Elias barked, "What?"

"What's going on with you?" Jacob moved into the wheelhouse beside him, using an overhead handhold to steady himself.

Eyes trained on the surf-splashed window, Elias muttered, "Nothing."

"Liar," Jacob countered.

They'd been crew mates for almost two decades, and best friends since childhood. Elias was frankly surprised it had taken Jacob this long to address his captain's growing surliness.

"It's not like the crew is hurting for cash," Jacob continued. "Missing the opening wouldn't be a big deal, so we're out here for something else. Maybe something to do with Lana Gregory?"

Elias's jaw twitched. Even the mention of her name made hormones flood his system. His need to claim her was becoming a real problem. He sighed and adjusted the throttle again as the boat nosed into a trough. "This isn't the time to get into that conversation."

"So that's a yes."

"I said not now." A wave surged over the bow, roaring like thunder and making the entire vessel shudder.

"You keep crashing into those waves like you are, there may not be a later." Jacob steadied himself against the dash. "Is she your mate?"

Elias scowled and nodded curtly.

"Fuck, man, how long have you known?"

"First day I met her." *And every fucking day since.* Kenai was a tiny community, and he seemed to run into Lana with disturbing frequency.

Jacob let out a low whistle. "You been holding back this whole time? Why? You got better game than that, man."

He knew he had better "game," as Jacob said, but he'd quickly discovered the company of other women didn't dampen his need for Lana. Which only made his seal more surly. But Elias had his principles, and he wasn't about to let what amounted to a biological urge run his or anyone else's life. "I won't steal another man's woman."

"Some selkie you are. Our ancestors would have whisked her off to a secluded island and had their way with her."

"This isn't the old days, and Lana's not the type to appreciate that sort of thing. She was loyal to Peter, and I admire that, even if he was a jerk." He turned the rudder to keep them on the upside of a swell.

Jacob grunted, adjusting his stance as the deck tilted. "If you hadn't been such an asshole all these years—"

"I was never an asshole to her. Only to her dickhead husband."

"I'm just saying she might have listened to you and I could be back at the bar right now, hitting on the hot new barmaid." Jacob scratched below his jaw, fingers rasping against his beard. "So now we're out here to do what?"

"If something happens, I want to be on hand to help. The *Willy Nilly* isn't cut out for these waves."

Leaning over the radar screen, Jacob pointed at the dot that was Lana's boat. "That her?"

"Yeah." The pit of Elias's stomach felt hollow as he thought of her in danger.

"Why's she so close to shore?"

"No idea. But I have a feeling something's wrong."

Jacob shrugged and jerked a thumb over his shoulder toward the door. "All right. Go keep an eye on deck, then. If there's trouble, you'll want to be in the water. I'll take the helm."

Elias paused only a moment, then nodded gratefully. He should've known Jacob would have his back. "Thanks."

Kicking out of his boots and clothing until all he wore was his sealskin vest, he exited the wheelhouse onto the rain-slick deck. His sealskin melded against his skin, growing and sliding over his limbs, protecting him from the driving rain and wind. Once they were in sight of the Willy Nilly, he'd shift into full seal form.

For now, he gripped the rail as the deck heaved and tossed under his feet, squinting at the horizon and hoping he was wrong about Lana heading toward danger.

CHAPTER FOUR

*L*ana gripped the wheel, her attention split between the horizon and the electronic navigation chart on her dashboard. Peter's grandfather had been a pro on these waters, and when Peter had inherited the boat, the only electronic devices had been a CB radio and the winch control for the net. She liked the idea of sensing the fish, of going with her gut, but after a couple of trips using only the GPS on Peter's phone, Peter had installed a more reliable system—one that wouldn't run out of battery, lose cell connection, or fall overboard. And she had to admit the fishing had improved. If nothing else, it made getting back to port easier.

Right now, however, something seemed off about her heading. She could see the vague, dark shape of the far shore, but her map was telling her she was at least four miles out. Her intuition told her this was all wrong; she shouldn't be able to see anything from here.

She pulled her cell phone from the pocket of her hoodie and opened her navigation app. The screen cycled as the app tried to connect, then popped up a message to try again later.

That's it, I'm turning around. She adjusted the rudder, taking a wave a bit too sharply, and heard a yelp from the crew cabin below as the deck tipped violently.

Jeanette poked her head up through the hatch. "Everything okay?"

"Navigation's not working. I'm heading back to port."

The deckhand crawled the rest of the way up the stairs and looked at the LCD display on the dashboard. "The wind out there is brutal. Maybe the antenna got knocked down."

Lana gritted her teeth. Sometimes she felt like the entire boat was held together by nothing more than duct tape and zip ties. "Maybe. Tell Joe to go look, please."

Jeanette scrunched up her face. "He's in the head, puking. I'll go."

Fuck. Joe was new this year, and despite his claim to have a ton of experience with a crew on the Bering Sea, he didn't actually appear to have a seaman's fortitude.

Jeanette, while great at picking fish from the net, was hardly bigger than a scrawny twelve-year-old; she'd get blown off the deck like a kite. "I'll go look. Take the rudder."

Grabbing her rain slicker and a flotation vest from a peg near the door, Lana headed outside into the storm. The rolling deck sent her stumbling toward the pole holding the antenna aloft. She gripped the thick rope looped along the cabin's outer wall and squinted upward against the rain. The antenna was still in place, but the navigation lights mounted below it were out.

A froth of saltwater rushed over the rail. She held on tightly until it subsided, then scanned the bundle of wires zip tied against the pole. Where the wires bent to enter a hole into the cabin, the plastic coating looked frayed, exposing the metal wires.

"God damnit," she swore as she turned back toward the cabin door. When had that happened? No way to fix it on the fly.

The boat listed steeply, and she gripped the rope with both hands, its rough fibers biting into her palms. Heading back to port was a good idea all the way around. The boat righted itself, and she stumbled forward. The door to the cabin was only a few steps away when a wall of saltwater slammed into her from behind. She was ripped from the guide rope and thrown to the deck. Her breath left her, and the shock of icy water made inhaling impossible for a moment. She flung her arms out, seeking something to hold on to as she slithered across the deck.

Her shoulder slammed into the rail on the far side, the blow softened by the padding of her life vest. Gasping, she grappled for purchase, palms slipping along the wet metal.

In a tilting rush, the water swept her up and over the side.

She plunged below the surface for a horrifying second before her flotation vest shot her upward again. Choking on salt water, she fought to keep her head above the swells.

"Jeanette!" she screamed. Had anyone even realized she'd gone over?

Limbs stiff with cold, she released the clasps on her waders, kicking free before they filled with water and dragged her under. Even so, the current sucked at her as she tried to swim toward the *Willy Nilly*. The waves were determined to drive them apart, and the wind seemed to hit her from every direction.

She sucked in a lungful of air just before a frothing gray wave rolled her under. When she surfaced again, the boat had disappeared. Spinning, she searched the undulating surface, finally seeing the boat crest a distant swell. Her chest constricted.

I'm going to die out here.

A vision of Elias telling her to stay put until the storm passed swept through her mind. If only she'd listened to the asshole. Even in summer, Alaska's ocean wasn't a place to go swimming; her arms and legs were already stiff with cold. Buoyed by her flotation vest, she bobbed like a cork, head under a wave then out again in unpredictable order. Her teeth chattered, and her eyes burned with salt water. With each passing second, her mind grew more addled as her heart struggled to keep blood flowing to her brain.

The swell she'd been riding seemed to drop out from under her like a roller coaster, leaving her stomach behind. She slid downward, an involuntary scream ripped from her lungs. Then she plunged below the surface, unable to tell up from down. Churning darkness surrounded her. Clutching her life vest, she squeezed her eyes shut, waiting for it to turn her upright again. Her lungs felt ready to burst.

When she was almost ready to give up, something solid hit her, driving her upward.

She broke the surface, choking and gasping, and tried to clear her eyes of the burning water. Something had hooked the back of her life vest and was dragging her along the waves. Her ass and legs bumped something warm below the surface. God, she wanted to turn around and latch onto it like a hot water bottle.

Unable to twist her head to see, she groped through the icy water below her, fingertips encountering sleek fur and lithe muscles. *A seal?*

The animal torpedoed forward, dragging her along like a rider on a runaway horse. Taking shallow breaths, she closed her eyes against the surging water. She had no idea what was happening, but didn't have the strength to figure anything out. Even with the adrenaline coursing through her and the seal's added warmth, her body was numb. The powerful urge to sleep made it difficult to stay conscious.

As long as the creature didn't decide to drag her to the bottom, she had no reason to fight it. And right now, it felt like the only thing keeping her alive.

Elias had plunged into the water the moment the *Willy Nilly's* mayday call crackled over the radio. His selkie senses could guide him to his destined mate more surely than the *Utkin's* radar. But now, with neither boat in sight, he was left with few options to get Lana to safety. She'd gone limp, and he knew the frigid ocean was taking its toll.

Keeping her head above water, he swam as hard as he could toward shore. He had to get her out of the water and warmed up immediately. Teeth aching from his grip on her life vest, he battled the current with his powerful flippers. *Faster, damn it.* A craggy beach lay a short distance ahead, but the waves crashing against the dark rocks made his approach difficult.

Even so, he dragged her forward, shielding her with his own body as the surging waves veered him off course and drove him against the protruding rocks. He slammed against stone and scraped barnacle-crusted boulders. By the time he reached the narrow ledge of gravel that marked the beach, he was bleeding and sore. Luckily, shifters healed fast. The moment his flippers touched the bottom, he shifted to human form and scooped Lana out of the water.

Cradling her against his chest, he carried her out of the white-capped surf. The wind drove his breath away and made it difficult to keep his eyes open as he limped toward a line of deformed spruce trees. Lana felt like dead weight in his arms. Her skin was icy pale, and her lips were blue. Even the skin beneath her eyes looked dark. He lowered her onto the moss at the base of a trunk, the overarching evergreen providing a decent shelter from the pounding rain.

He laid his fingers against her throat, finding her pulse. It was weak, and her chest moved slightly as she inhaled. *Alive.* Relief rushed through him. But he was concerned that she wasn't shivering. If she was cold enough to stop shivering, it might already be too late.

Without a fire or even a real shelter from the elements, there was only one option—body heat.

"Don't you die on me, Lana," he muttered as he pulled off the life vest and wrestled her sodden cotton hoodie and jeans free. He shrugged out of his sealskin vest and willed it to expand until it was the size of a blanket. No human had ever seen him without his pelt in one form or another. It was a part of him as much as his eyes or hands. Without it, he lost his power. Couldn't shift.

He lay next to Lana on the moss and pulled the fur over them both, tucking the edge in around her knees and shoulders. Her frame felt frail and cold as he spooned against her, pulling her close. She let out a tiny sigh and seemed to settle against him, as if unconsciously recognizing she was finally where she belonged.

Beneath the salt water dampening her hair and skin, she smelled like cinnamon. His body was responding to her nearness with embarrassing intensity, and his inner seal was doing backflips of delight.

He wrapped both arms firmly around her and tried not to think about the lacy red bra and plain cotton panties she wore. Of course her underthings wouldn't match. She probably dressed with the same spontaneity and lack of planning she displayed with the rest of her activities. Of all the people in the world who could have been his mate, fate had paired him with his complete opposite.

Unfortunately, the mating attraction didn't guarantee a happily-ever-after. Few of the old stories about selkies kidnapping their human mates ended well; inevitably, the selkie returned to the sea alone. Elias was already doomed to spend the rest of his days pining for a woman who hated him. There was no reason for him to compound the matter by claiming her. As a human, at least Lana could remain blissfully unaware of the empty angst an unfulfilled bond created.

As they lay there, her breathing grew deeper and her skin warmed. Relief filled him. She would be all right. He let his fingers trace up the soft skin of her stomach, but stopped himself before he reached the swell of her breast. *Damn it all for fate putting me—putting us—here.* Together, nearly naked, a thing of his dreams.

Closing his eyes, he balled his hands into fists and focused on his breathing. The last thing he needed was for her to accuse him of taking advantage of her. Once he was absolutely certain she would be all right, he would slip away and swim for help. He should probably go now, before she woke, but her clothes were wet, and there could be bears nearby. Plus, who knew what she might do if she woke up all alone? Better to make sure she was safe and alert.

His seal hounded him in his mind. Images of her rolling over and straddling him, of her settling her heat over his pelvis, of exquisite pleasure as she lowered her heat over his shaft made him groan out loud. *That will never happen*, he told his seal.

Even so, he drifted off to sleep dreaming of clamping his teeth to her shoulder in the bite that would bond them for life.

Whether they liked each other or not.

CHAPTER FIVE

A draft roused Lana, and she rolled over, reaching to adjust the blanket. Her fingertips met coarse fur rather than the soft fleece she expected. Her eyes popped open. A mosaic of branches blocked out most of the gray sky overhead. The sound of pattering rain and wind reached her, but where she lay remained dry and blissfully warm.

It took a moment for everything to come back to her; the frayed navigation wires, the fall overboard, the bone-numbing cold. Her mind was fuzzy about the details, but she thought she'd been rescued by a seal…

To her left, someone was snoring softly. She turned her head, finding dark, silver streaked hair, a stubbled jaw, and a familiar scar bisecting his eyebrow. "Elias?" She recoiled, kicking free of the heavy fur blanket and rolling away. Cold air hit her skin, and she looked down to find herself in nothing but her bra and panties. "What the fuck?"

Elias opened his dark eyes and stretched as if he woke like this every morning of his life. His chest was bare, broadly muscled with a dusting of hair that tapered to a line that disappeared beneath the silver and black spotted sealskin drawn up over his hips. His gaze raked her body, and she swore a hint of a smile pulled at his mouth. "Lana."

Kneeling on the damp moss, she crossed her arms around her torso as she looked around for her clothing. She and Elias were under the thick boughs of a wind-battered spruce tree, and the sound of the surf crashing into rocks told her they were near shore. But where?

The ground sloped upward toward the tree, rain-darkened stones forming an irregular protected hollow around the trunk. Piles of her sodden clothing lay strewn across the ground nearby. "Why am I naked?"

"You were hypothermic. I didn't have a way to start a fire, so…" He shrugged and glanced down at his chest, then looked at her with raised eyebrows as if that explained everything.

She scowled. He had a point. "Body heat. Fine. But how are you here?"

Elias remained lying on the moss, disconcertingly comfortable, considering the situation. "Your crew sent out a distress call. I came to save you."

She stared at him wide-eyed. She hadn't seen his boat, but it could've been out of sight among the huge waves as she was tossed around. She'd been separated from the *Willy Nilly* in a matter of minutes. "But how did you end up in the water?"

His gaze met hers with an intensity that made her want to squirm. "I couldn't stand by and watch you drown."

Her throat felt tight, and she dropped her gaze. She didn't like feeling beholden to anyone, let alone Elias Sobol, but here she was. "Thank you."

She picked up her sodden hoodie and retrieved her cell phone from the pocket. The OtterBox case had protected the phone from water, but the battery was dead. She'd had at least half a charge on it last she checked, but the cold could've sapped it faster. How long had they been out here? She rubbed her forehead and squinted beneath the boughs at the rain. The monochrome gray daylight made it impossible to judge what time it was. "Dammit, my phone is dead. Do you have any idea where we are?"

"Nope. I was just happy to find land."

"Shit. I wonder how far the current carried us." The tides in the inlet came and went with a vengeance, sucking everything out to sea.

She gathered her other clothing, feeling his gaze follow her every move. The asshole was enjoying this, but she couldn't exactly be ungrateful. He'd gone overboard to save her, and now he was stranded here, too. "Where are your clothes?"

He adjusted the vest draped over his hips, which somehow seemed smaller than before. "I, um, dropped them down on the beach."

Wringing out her t-shirt as best as she could, she tugged it over her head. An involuntary shiver coursed through her. July in Alaska could get downright cold when the clouds blocked the sun, and the wind cut into her like a knife. "Brrr."

"You're going to get hypothermia again," Elias said, his voice husky. "Come back under the fur."

Her stomach fluttered, and for a moment, she was tempted to do just that. She hadn't been touched since her single night with Cal, and it was as if her skin craved human contact. She shook off the desire. Was she feeling like this because she owed him, or was something going on with her hormones? She wanted nothing to do with Elias Sobol, even if he was the last man on Earth.

She swallowed, realizing he *could* be the last human being she ever saw. People got lost in the Alaskan wilderness all the time, never to be found. *Not gonna happen, Lana.* They were going to be rescued. Two ships missing crew meant there would be all that many more people looking for them. She just needed to build a signal fire.

She looked around for her boots but didn't see them, vaguely recalling that she'd kicked them off along with her waders while she'd been in the water. Locating her jeans, she wrung them out. "We can't just lie around and expect to be rescued. We need a signal fire or something."

Elias rose, and she couldn't help gawking. He had the body of an underwear model—*without the underwear.* His heavily muscled thighs tapered to lean hips, and from the tuft of hair between his legs he sported a good-sized semi that made her wonder what he'd look like fully erect. He pulled the sealskin up and she recognized his vest. He hesitated a moment, and she lifted her gaze from his crotch to find him smirking.

Heat filled her face. *What is wrong with me?* Turning away, she shoved her legs into her clammy, salt-crusted jeans. "I'm going to the beach to see if I can tell where we are."

"I'll come with you."

Shoeless, she minced away from the shelter of the trees. Without the spruce's protection, the rain fell hard enough to rebound off the ground, sending droplets raining upward. *So much for wringing out my clothes.* She shivered under the deluge. If the air turned any colder, it would hail.

Elias had somehow managed to twist his fur vest into a kilt around his waist. Now he looked like some sexy savage caveman in a fur loincloth as they moved toward the sound of the crashing surf. She wanted to slap herself upside the head for the lewd thoughts she was having, but instead hurried forward until she reached a minuscule beach of gray silt. Within a few feet, it transitioned to waves frothing around jagged stones. The shore to either side rose into sharp cliffs.

Rain blew sideways against her, making it difficult to breathe, but she blinked away the water streaming from her hair into her eyes and scanned the horizon. Rescue planes and helicopters would be grounded in this weather, and even boats were probably finding shelter. *What was I thinking, bringing the Willy Nilly out in this?* She squinted along the beach in search of Elias's things. "I don't see your clothes."

He shaded his eyes from the rain and gave the shoreline a cursory glance. "Must've washed away in the storm." He turned away from the water and held a hand toward her. "We should go back to the shelter and wait this out."

The storm-bruised sky had darkened, signaling sunset. He was right, but she didn't want to admit it. And she definitely didn't want to hold his hand. She wrapped her arms around her torso and shook her head. "I can make it on my own."

His eyes hardened, and he dropped his hand. "Suit yourself."

She let him take several steps before she followed him back to the hollow beneath the spruce tree. Elias sat against the trunk, meeting her gaze with a challenge as his bulk took up most of the compact space. There was no way to avoid physical contact. She was growing colder by the minute, each breath making her chest ache. *Fuck it*. Grudgingly, she sat next to him.

"You're shivering again." He put his arm around her shoulders and pulled her close. "We need to keep each other warm."

She stiffened, a protest on her lips. Then his heat hit her and she melted into it with a grateful shudder. "How are you so warm?"

"Practice, I guess. My dad used to toss us into the surf as kids. Said it would acclimate us to a life at sea."

"That sounds awful." She shook her head. "I'm one of those people who dip a toe in first and then take twenty minutes to get my hair wet."

He chuckled, the rumble making her insides flutter. She'd expected his vest to smell like a wet dog, but he smelled rather pleasant, warm and musky with a hint of pine that probably came from the tree behind them.

Looking for a change of subject, she asked, "You think they'll find us?"

If the sun was setting, they'd been missing for at least twelve hours. Anything more than twenty-four, and rescue crews no longer looked for survivors; they looked for bodies.

"We just need to stay alive until they do." He rested his cheek against the top of her head, a familiar gesture she shouldn't be comfortable accepting. But he was so *warm*.

"I can't believe I'm stuck here with you of all people," she grumbled.

A low, rumbling chuckle rolled from his chest again. "I'm not as bad as your husband made me out to be."

Peter. He'd been jealous of every man who glanced her direction, especially Elias. She knew it wasn't because she was some magnificent beauty, with her splotchy red cheeks and mousy brown hair that bordered on frizzy. But Peter had made her feel beautiful. *He made all the women he met feel beautiful.* She shoved down that thought, refusing to think ill of the dead. She'd never caught him cheating, but she knew he had. And Elias Sobol was way more of an asshole than Peter'd ever been. *No fucking way am I going to go soft on Elias, not even under these circumstances.*

Summoning every ounce of her willpower, she drew away, regretting the cold draft that came between them. "I guess if we ever get out of here alive, I owe you one."

Turning her back to him, she curled up on the moss and pretended to sleep.

CHAPTER SIX

*E*lias lay stiffly beside Lana, listening to her breathing. He'd thought for a moment she was softening toward him. That he had a chance of showing her he wasn't the bad guy her husband had painted him to be. *I shouldn't have brought up her husband.* It was obvious she had no idea Peter had cheated on her, and far be it from Elias to besmirch the memory of a dead man. Not that she'd believe Elias about anything. He could spend a hundred years trying to prove he wasn't a villain, and she'd still give him the cold shoulder.

Being marooned with her wasn't going to heal their relationship. And the more time he spent near her, the more his selkie nature wanted to keep her here, all to himself, whether she liked him or not. He needed to go before both he and his seal did something they couldn't take back.

Once he was sure Lana was asleep, he covered her with her raincoat to hold in what little warmth she had, and slipped away. He would've left her his pelt, but he needed it if he was going to swim for help. Too bad selkies didn't have long-distance telepathy with their clan members like other shifters, or he'd call his crew. It would take him hours to get back to the peninsula, and more hours to rally a rescue team.

Wading into the surf, he adjusted his pelt and let the shift take hold. As always, the faint shimmer of magic rose all around him while his limbs shortened and his legs fused. He shrugged off the discomfort as his face extended, whiskers sprouting from his nose. The fur melded against him and spread, insulating him from the frigid water, until he was once more in his sleek selkie body.

Diving below the surface, he weaved his way between the rocks and headed east, his internal compass directing him toward home. Jacob would be patrolling the water in the area, hopefully catching salmon while he waited for Elias to come back. Diesel wasn't cheap, and it would be nice to bring in enough of a catch to at least break even on this fiasco of a trip.

After swimming for about an hour, Elias sensed the presence of his crew nearby and popped his head above the surface. Searching the twilight until he spotted the lights of the *Utkin* in the distance, he sent a mental signal to his crew and dove through the rolling swells toward the boat. Once he was alongside the hull, he transformed back into a man and climbed the rungs welded to the side.

The entire crew stood on deck to meet him, the harsh lights mounted outside the cabin illuminating their concerned faces. Jacob gave him a hand over the gunnel, his eyebrows drawn into a frown. "I take it you didn't find her?"

Elias balanced on the heaving deck. The storm had abated, but rain still sputtered and the seas were rough. "I towed her to one of the islands. She was hypothermic, but she's okay now." He strode toward the wheelhouse. "We can send the skiff out to retrieve her."

"So," Jacob said, trailing close at his heels, the rest of the crew trailing behind him. "Do we have a new clan member?"

"No," Elias said tersely.

The crew grumbled with discontent—obviously Jacob had told them everything. Now the men would hound him for eternity. He just wanted to forget any of this had ever happened.

He redirected the conversation. "How's the *Willy Nilly?*"

"They had to be towed back to port—some sort of trouble with their navigation system—but the crew is fine," Jacob answered.

Someone elbowed Elias in the kidney, and he turned to discover all four crewmen had piled into the wheelhouse behind him.

He scowled. "What the hell?"

"Jacob told us she's your mate," Bobby said, shaking rain from his dark hair. He had to hunch to keep his head from bumping the ceiling. "Now we understand why you've been such a pain in the ass the last two seasons."

Walton added, "We wanna hear how it went."

"She hates me, that's how." Elias pulled up the navigation charts. "Now let's get this rescue mission over with."

"You have her all to yourself!" Bobby said. "Why aren't you still with her?"

Dean scratched his head. "And how can you explain suddenly showing up in the *Utkin's* skiff?"

Elias glared over his shoulder at the wolf shifter. "She'll be grateful for a rescue. I doubt she's going to care how it comes along. I'll tell her I was on the beach and flagged you down."

Walton glowered at him from beneath his sealskin hat. "You need to go back."

"Spend more time with her," Bobby added. "This is your chance to claim her."

"I just want to get this over with and go back to having her hate me from afar," Elias growled.

Jacob crossed his arms. "Nope. Sorry, bro. I'm with the guys on this one. You have a mate, which is more than any of us can say. You're going to go back and deal with this."

Elias rounded on them, using his Alpha voice. "Who's captain here? Me. I call the shots. Now get out so I can chart our course."

Jacob raised one eyebrow and glanced at the other men.

Elias narrowed his gaze, feeling them cut him out of the mental connection. Among selkies, not only was the mental connection not as strong as it was for other shifters, an Alpha's power wasn't as undeniable. Today, it seemed his crew was going to ignore it.

Bobby shrugged and took a step forward. "Let's do it."

In a surge of motion, the men took hold of Elias.

"What the fuck?" He struggled as they dragged him from the pilot's cabin and into the blowing rain. "Let go of me."

They hauled him toward the rail. "I won't stand for this."

As a single unit, they tossed him over.

Instinct turned his fall into a dive, and he entered the water smoothly, resurfacing a few feet away. He didn't change his form, just tread water and glowered up at his crew standing along the rail. "This is mutiny," he shouted.

Jacob laughed. "Call it mutiny if you want, but we're not letting you back on board until you and Lana kiss and make up."

Elias bared his teeth, struggling to find a decent argument. "I don't have any survival gear. She could die out there."

"Don't give me that bullshit." Jacob crossed his arms. "I was with you in Prince William Sound. You know how to survive." He was referring to the summer after high school, when they'd decided to embrace their selkie side and live off the land. For two months, they'd lived like wild things until they both decided they missed pizza and returned home.

Bobby grinned at him. "Women love that hunter gatherer shit. Go prove you're a worthy mate."

Jacob backed away from the rail. "Get out of here, Elias. We have fish to catch before the run dies down. I have a feeling we're going to need the money for wedding presents."

The other men nodded and smirked. There would be no getting back on board the *Utkin*. He could swim all the way back to Kenai and report Lana's location to the Coast Guard, but that would mean a lot of explaining that wouldn't correspond to Lana's version of things. He was going to have to come up with an alternate plan. But while he did that, he had to make sure Lana was taken care of.

He gave his men a final, withering look and shifted to his seal form.

Their laughter followed him as he dove through the water back toward the island.

CHAPTER SEVEN

*L*ana woke shivering. Elias's heat was missing. She drew her knees toward her chest and huddled beneath her raincoat, waiting for him to come back. A few minutes stretched into a half an hour. She sat up and called for him but received no answer. Where'd he gone?

Never very good at waiting, she rose and shoved her arms into her hoodie's damp sleeves, adding her raincoat on top. She ducked out from under the branches. The rain and the wind had stopped, but the morning air felt like she'd opened a freezer door. "Elias!"

The shush of the waves and the cry of an early morning gull were all that answered. Suddenly faced with the thought of being stranded alone, she climbed the nearby rocks to get a better look around. A rivulet of water cut its way through the spongy terrain toward the beach, making her realize that her mouth felt like cotton. Tempted as she was to drink, she knew better than to consume runoff. Hopefully, this was a spring, and she could trace it to its source. Maybe Elias had gone looking for water?

She followed the path upward, warming a little with the activity. Conscious there might be bears around, she sang one of her favorite church songs; the peaceful morning silence felt too pristine to belt out a favorite from the top forty, as she usually did while she worked on the boat.

The sun hovered just below the horizon, a sliver of orange sky showing beneath a blanket of thick clouds. It seemed the storm was moving away and that bit of open sky was headed her direction. She continued upward, walking carefully to avoid hurting her bare feet on the rocks and brush, until she reached a puddle the size of a washbasin at the foot of an upthrust boulder. The runnel of water she'd been following seemed to begin here, and she fell to her knees in gratitude. It should be safe to drink at the source.

The cold, clean water burned and soothed her dry throat, and it was difficult to limit herself to a few swallows. But if it would upset her stomach, she was better off not overdoing it. She washed the grime from her hands and face, then stood and looked around.

Elias obviously hadn't come this way. So where had he gone?

Her climb had carried her above the tree line, and the bald, stony top of the island rose another hundred feet or so above her. Below, the jagged cliffs and overhanging brush formed a shallow protected cradle around the beach where she and Elias had come to shore. The wind had died down, but the morning air was still quite chilling, and she longed for the radiant heat of Elias inside their shelter.

Bare feet aching, she climbed the rest of the way to the top to look over the rest of the island. All she saw was rocks and grass. "Elias!" she shouted, searching the rocks and crags for movement. Far below, where the tide had subsided, sharp boulders poked from the exposed mudflats. A boat would not be able to get very close to the island with so many obstacles. It was a miracle she and Elias had reached shore without being bashed to death.

There was no sign of Elias, only a few angry gulls protecting their nests. One bird swooped dangerously close to her, forcing her to duck. Knowing gulls could be quite fearsome, she hurried back down the slope before she lost an eye, still searching the area for Elias. Part of her wondered if she'd hallucinated his presence the same way she'd imagined he was a seal when they were in the water.

Regardless of whether she could find Elias or not, she needed to build a fire, and she needed to find food. All she had was a tiny pocketknife that had been her dad's and was more of a talisman than a tool. She patted her jeans pocket to be certain it was still there. Maybe she could whittle herself a fishing spear or something.

Passing the shelter, she continued on until she reached the beach, now a long mudflat dotted by rocks. She looked at her bare feet, toes cold against the ground, and saw the distinctive dimple in the mud that told her a clam was beneath her. Elated at the thought of food, she selected a thin bit of driftwood and set out to dig, careful to pay attention to her footing. The coastal silt in Alaska could be as deadly as the water itself, grabbing hold of unwary feet and refusing to let go until the incoming tide drowned the victim.

At the next dimple, she shoved the thin stick into it. In theory, the clam would close around the stick and root itself in place while she dug. After a few minutes and a lot of mud, her fingertips met the familiar sharp edge of a razor clam. Digging furiously, she pulled it free. It was lovely, about the size of her hand with an olive green shell, and her stomach rumbled as she imagined warm clam chowder. Then she grimaced, remembering that she not only didn't have butter or milk, she didn't have a fire to cook the thing.

Worry about that later. She stuffed it into the pocket of her raincoat and carried on, capturing two more clams before she reached the water.

Feeling pleased with herself, she turned toward shore.

While she'd been preoccupied, the incoming tide had blocked her off, leaving her standing on a boulder-strewn stretch of silt. She hurried her steps, fighting the cold mud sucking at her naked ankles. The ground was getting softer and softer as the water rose, and she tried to stay near the rocky areas. At one point, she took a step and sank halfway up her shin. Her momentum threw her forward onto her hands and knees. Gritty saltwater splashed into her eyes, blinding her as she struggled to stand, and pain lanced through her ankle. When she tried to put weight on it, white-hot agony made her cry out. *Shit shit shit.*

"I did not survive going overboard only to die in the mud like some landlubber," she chided herself and kept limping forward, each step forcing her to whimper.

When she reached the channel separating her from the shore, she paused only a moment. Thirty or forty feet separated her from safety, silty water roiling as the water moved in. There was no option except forward. She waded in, the chill not as bad as she'd expected, probably because she was already cold and covered in mud. *It can't be that deep*, she told herself. It wasn't as if she'd climbed a hill on her way out, just a slight dip in the ground. As the water hit her thighs, her ankle gave out.

Arms flailing, she plunged below the surface.

She surfaced, gasped for air, and was rolled under again. She didn't have a life vest on this time, and her raincoat tangled around her, hindering her movement. *This can't be happening. Not again.* She couldn't get her bearings to swim toward shore.

Then powerful hands had her by the shoulders. Her head broke the surface, and she gulped in air. Blinking away seawater, her legs churned the water as Elias dragged her onto shore. He set her down on the hard gravel and knelt beside her. "What the hell were you trying to do, walk back to the mainland?"

She coughed and spluttered, unable to respond for a few moments. Of course the asshole had to try to make her sound stupid. Finally, she rasped out, "You're a dick, you know that?"

"I just saved you. Again." He sat back on his heels to glare at her. "How does that make me a dick?"

"Of course I wasn't trying to walk to the mainland. I was digging clams. Getting us *food*. Where the hell were you?" She sat up, glaring at him.

His expression turned thoughtful. "You're right, that wasn't a nice thing for me to say."

The ire burning a hole in her chest cooled. At least he was willing to admit he'd been a jerk. A gust of wind cut through her wet clothing and she shivered. The mud had been bad enough, but being wet again was sapping the last of her energy reserves. She started to get her legs under her, but then her ankle flexed and she winced. "Fuck."

"What is it?"

Through gritted teeth, she shook her head and said, "I twisted my ankle."

He placed a gentle hand on her calf. "Better let me look."

She sucked in a breath as he edged up the cuff of her wet jeans. Her ankle hurt, but she was also highly aware that wherever he brushed her bare skin, tendrils of electricity raced straight to her belly button. *This is not romantic, you idiot*. Yet heat still pooled between her legs. She tried to remind herself how much she hated him, despite the way his gentle touch was making her feel all melty inside. Then he rotated her foot a fraction, and she yelped, all heat vanishing in a wash of agony.

"Sorry." He looked up at her with concern. "I don't think it's broken, but you should keep your weight off it until we're rescued. Let's go back to the tree where its dry." He slid his arms under her knees and shoulders, lifting her before she could react.

Lana instinctively wrapped both arms around his neck, welcoming the heat from his body. "We won't get rescued by hiding in the trees." She glanced over his shoulder toward the ocean. "We need to build a fire so someone can see us from a distance."

"How do you propose we do that?" He slowed his gait to look at her but didn't stop.

Intensely aware that his mouth was close enough to kiss, she took a fluttery breath. His masculine pine scent gave her the unaccountable urge to trace the scar over his eyebrow with her fingertips. *Stop being a dodo and focus.* She forced her gaze away from his to search the rock-strewn beach. "Look for fool's gold. I used to find it on the beach all the time when Mom and Dad took me camping."

He stopped and turned around to face the water. "How will fool's gold help us make fire?"

"I have a pocketknife." She dug in her jeans pocket and pulled it out. "We can strike them together to make sparks."

His brows arched. "You keep surprising me."

An intense heat flooded her cheeks, but she swallowed it away.

They'd moved inland past the high tide mark to where beach grass covered the sandy ground, and he lowered her gently next to a big hunk of driftwood. A moment of regret filled her as he pulled away. She wrapped her arms over her chest and tried not to shiver.

"Take off your raincoat," he said.

"Why?" Her arms and torso felt waterlogged under her raincoat, but if she took it off, the wind would feel even more biting.

His hands were already removing the sealskin from his waist. She found herself unable to look away from his movements as he pulled it free and held it out to her, holding the fur in a way that strategically blocked her view of a full frontal. "You're cold. Put this on."

"But—"

"I'll cover myself with your raincoat."

She was going to ask if he would get cold, but her words dried up as he bent to lay the fur over her lap, giving her the view she'd been waiting for. Just as thick as she remembered, the masculinity between his muscular thighs warmed her core, even if her fingers and toes were tingly and numb. Gulping, she shrugged out of her raincoat, feeling like a klutz as the wet hoodie underneath bunched up and refused to let the sleeves loose.

"Let me help." Moving behind her, he eased both sleeves free. "You should take off that cotton hoodie, too."

When he stepped out from behind her again, he'd wrapped the raincoat around his hips, one thigh exposed under the knotted sleeves, but the most important parts were covered.

Lana didn't understand how he stayed warm, but she needed to focus on something besides his near nakedness. She remembered the clams she'd gathered. *At least I'm not entirely useless.* "Check the pockets. I put the clams in there."

He checked both, but the clams were gone, probably swept away when she fell into the water.

Her heart fell. "Dammit."

"It's okay. I caught a fish." He pointed down the beach.

A large orange rockfish lay on the gray silt. Of course he'd one-upped her and caught fish. And rockfish was her favorite. Her stomach rumbled, and Elias chuckled. "Sit tight. I'll go look for fool's gold."

He strode down the beach, looking as comfortable in her raincoat as he'd been in the fur, which was now warming her with surprising efficiency. She peeled out of the hoodie and pulled the sealskin up to her chin.

Elias was a big guy, and the long vest covered her like a blanket.

She sighed. Perhaps Elias Sobol wasn't all bad. He'd saved her from drowning—twice—provided food, kept her warm, and now was going to build her a fire. She'd even gotten him to admit he was a dick. Without his help, she'd have been dead already. As she watched him search the beach, she resolved to give him the benefit of the doubt from now on.

CHAPTER EIGHT

*E*lias had never left his pelt unattended, let alone given it over to someone, and he'd never felt as defenseless as he did right now. His seal should be uncomfortable, too, but remained remarkably silent on the matter as Elias scoured the beach for anything that looked like fool's gold. Perhaps whatever part of his spirit animal inhabited the pelt was now happily snuggling up to his mate. He glanced at Lana as a silly twang of jealousy hurried him on his search.

Soon, he spotted a stone the size of a flattened softball with angular edges that caught the light with a metallic sheen. He pried it from the silt and carried it toward Lana, detouring to rescue the rockfish from some hungry seagulls on the way.

She'd pulled the sealskin up to her chin, and he liked seeing her wrapped in it. He lay the fish down near her and she sat up. Through her wet tee shirt, her nipples jutted like small shells, and his groin hardened. If he wasn't careful, his arousal would become embarrassing under the raincoat.

He forced his gaze off her, looking at the stone in his hands and thinking about the task ahead. "Will this do?"

"I think so. Now we need firewood." She scanned the surrounding sand, leaning over to pick up a twig hardly bigger than her thumb. "I have to say, you aren't so bad to be stranded with."

His chest warmed, and his seal swam joyful circles through his mind. *Bring her more rocks!* He pushed his seal's advice aside, but Bobby's recommendation to do "hunter gatherer shit" floated into his head. He dropped the stone with a thump and hurried to a nearby pile of seaweed and other debris that had tangled around a big chunk of driftwood. Digging it from the mud, he heaved against the gray trunk, dragging it free.

"What are you doing?" Lana called.

Still bent over the butt end of the log, he looked over his shoulder at her. "Gathering firewood."

Lana looked at him like he was crazy. "Haven't you made a fire before? That thing will never burn. We need small, dry pieces." She held up her tiny piece of driftwood. "Kindling."

He let the wood fall back to the ground with a thump and ran a hand over his hair. He'd been around bonfires, but never taken part in starting one or even paid attention when someone else did. He was a selkie, after all, and spent most of his life on the water. All he knew was you threw wood on it—the bigger the better, from all he'd seen. "Guess I got a little carried away."

"Yeah, you could say that." She glanced at her bare, mud-crusted foot sticking out from under the edge of the fur. The delicate bones of her ankle showed definite signs of swelling. "I wish I could get up and help. I hate being useless."

"I can handle it. I just..." He understood her need to be useful, so even though he already felt vulnerable without his pelt, he admitted, "I've never built a fire before."

He expected her to scoff or make a cutting remark. The old Lana would have. Instead, her mouth dropped open. "Really? Never? I assumed you were the true-Alaskan-male outdoorsy type."

"I am. Just outdoors on the water, not on land."

She licked her lips, took a deep breath, and nodded slowly. "How about I tell you what to do and you handle the heavy lifting?"

Relief flooded him, and he dramatically flexed both biceps. "I'm at your command."

She laughed, a sound as tantalizing as a siren's song. Gods, how could the woman turn him to mush with the tiniest things? She stretched out an arm and picked up more of the little sticks within her reach. "First off, gather dry wood only. Not anything buried in seaweed. Most of the dry stuff will be small. Then get some dead grass for tinder. I saw tufts of it on the hill back there. Oh, and some twigs from the spruce tree. Those burn great."

He did as she asked and soon had a good-sized pile of useable firewood. Lana made a tiny nest of dry grass and twigs. Pulling her knife from her pocket, she began striking against the lump of fool's gold. Sure enough, sparks scattered every which way. A curl of smoke rose from the center of her arrangement. She bent low, blowing gently until tiny orange flames licked upward. She gave him a triumphant glance.

He nodded, feeling his eyes twinkle. She was sexy as hell when she was happy. "Good job."

She flushed, as if unused to getting compliments, her attention on the fire. "Only if I can keep it going."

As she fed wood to the growing flames, he picked up the fish. "If you're done with your knife, I'll clean our dinner."

"That would be awesome." She beamed. "I'm starving."

Accepting the knife, he went down to the water and cleaned the spiny fish. Skewering it on two sticks, he carried it back to the fire and propped it over the crackling flames. Soon, the savory smell of rockfish filled the air. The sun had risen and now glinted off the water, the soft lap of the waves a welcome difference to the crashing force they'd been yesterday.

"God, that smells good." Lana took a deep breath and poked at the blackening skin with a finger. "I think this part's done. Hand me my knife."

He rubbed the ivory handle with his thumb, examining the salmon etched into the surface before handing it over. "My grandpa had a knife like that, but bigger. I think it may have been the same artist."

She opened the blade. "My dad gave it to me the first time I went out on the boat with Peter. Said it would bring me luck." She snorted. "I don't think it works."

"Well, it's lucky you have it with you." He adjusted the sticks holding the fish so she could reach it more easily. "Maybe we make a good team after all."

Lana huffed a laugh. "Who'd've thought."

Well, it wasn't a passionate kiss, but it wasn't rejection, either. He watched her dig the blade into the side of the fish. "Why doesn't your dad fish with you?"

"He's not a fishing kind of guy." She pried up some flaky white meat. "He and Mom used to own Patty Cakes, the bakery. You know it?"

He nodded. Every shifter in Alaska had heard of Patty Cakes. The current owner, Lana's cousin, had helped solve the rogue mystery plaguing shifters across the state and had ended up becoming a shifter herself—an Alpha wolf who now ran a pack alongside her mate. Not that Lana would know that. Family or not, shifters didn't talk about magic with humans.

Lana continued, "Dad's got arthritis and the cold weather gets to him. He and Mom retired to Florida several years ago."

"How'd you end up on a fishing boat? I'm surprised you didn't take over the bakery," Elias said.

"I did for a while. But then I met Peter..." she tapered off, obviously not wanting to bring up a sore subject.

Why does it always have to come back to Peter? Did she know her husband had cheated on her, not just once, but over and over? His throat ached with the desire to tell her, but based on past interactions with her, he knew that would likely just make her jump to the dead man's defense. And he had to admit, he respected a woman who stayed true. But the ghost of her dead husband would always come between them.

Clearing his throat, he asked softly, "You loved him very much, didn't you?"

She didn't look at him, instead taking a bite of food and chewing slowly before answering. "He showed me how much I love the water. I'm addicted to the salt air and sun, the roll of the deck, the thrill of the catch. I could never go back to working in the bakery full time."

He remained silent, watching her. She hadn't said she loved Peter, only that he'd helped her find her passion. Did that mean Elias had a chance to win her heart? His seal flipped at the possibility.

She took another bite of the fish and moaned. "God, this is the best fish I've ever eaten."

Glad she'd changed the subject, he said, "You should try my cooking when I have access to a kitchen." He gestured toward the fire. "I'm not at my best over a campfire."

"I imagine not, since you've never started one." She chuckled, then added, "For some reason I have trouble picturing you in the kitchen."

He watched her lick her finger in a way he was certain was completely innocent, but that tightened his balls in anticipation. He reached for the fish and pulled it completely off the fire, laying it on a flat rock nearby. "Dad was always trying new recipes when I was a kid, especially ethnic ones."

"Your dad? Not your mom? Not that I'm judging, but you strike me as someone who comes from a more patriarchal background."

"Mom wasn't in the picture much. She ran off with another man when I was eleven." And was the reason he would never steal another man's wife. His mother and father hadn't been fated mates, but even so, Dad had never recovered from the abandonment.

"Oh." Lana's cheeks flushed. "Now I feel like an ass. Sorry if I dredged up something painful."

He shook his head and shot her a wry smile. Despite the touchy subject, he was enjoying the conversation. "It's all right. My dad and brothers are great. When we get back to land, I'll cook you a celebration dinner."

She seemed to consider a long moment. "I think I'd like that." Then she sighed and looked toward the ocean. "But we have to get rescued, first. I hope someone finds us soon."

He nodded in agreement, but felt his precious time alone with her slipping away.

CHAPTER NINE

*T*here were a thousand reasons why Lana should keep her distance from Elias Sobol. But the man sitting across the fire from her now was nothing like the adversary Peter had hated for most of their marriage. This Elias was thoughtful, funny, and honest. Was it only because they were marooned, or had she been blinded by Peter's bias?

The day passed without a single boat sighting across the gray horizon. As twilight darkened the sky, the wind picked up once more, chilling her even under Elias's warm fur vest.

The jeans and tee shirt she was wearing had dried, but the hoodie draped over the top of the driftwood log was still damp, and she loathed the idea of putting it back on. Her gaze kept drifting to Elias's sculpted chest and arms, and although he never complained about the cold, she couldn't help noticing his small nipples were hard. Guilt crept up her throat. *He has to be freezing.*

She gestured to the vest tucked around her body. "You should take this back."

His dark eyes met hers, glinting in the orange light of the flames. He looked almost savage, a dark scruff marking his square jaw. He put a hand on hers, stopping her from unwrapping the fur. "It's going to get colder before the sun comes up again. You keep it."

She glanced down at his hand, stomach going fluttery at his touch. She couldn't believe what she was about to say. "At least come sit under it with me. We can both stay warm."

His gaze grew sharper, and the fluttering in her belly dropped lower, settling between her thighs. Without a word, he scooted over, propping his back against the driftwood log beside her. She lifted the fur, letting in a rush of cool air, and he slid closer until his naked thigh pressed against her. Silly as it was, part of her wished her legs were bare, too, so she could feel his skin.

"Here," he said, lifting his arm over her head. His voice was soft and low, making her blood tingle.

She sat forward, and he put his arm around her shoulders, pulling her tightly against him. Maybe this wasn't such a good idea. But she couldn't take back the offer now. She readjusted, ankle aching but bearable.

His skin was slightly chilled as she rested her cheek against his chest, but he warmed quickly.

Other than her one-night-stand with Cal, she hadn't been this close to a man since before Peter died, and the intimacy sent a rush of pleasure through her. Trying to understand the weird feelings, she said, "I never imagined I'd be snuggled in front of a campfire with you of all people."

Turning his head, he rested his chin on top of her hair, making her nerves thrill even more. His voice rumbled from his chest, vibrating through her bones. "Is it so awful?"

She gulped and shook her head no against him.

He gave her a gentle squeeze. "Good."

They sat together for a while, watching the sky darken to indigo velvet. Elias pointed to a single bright pinprick of light just above the horizon. "Look, there's Venus."

Goddess of love, she thought but didn't say. What the hell was going on with her? The clouds had parted in places, and a flicker of green to the north caught her attention. "Holy shit, is that the northern lights? You never see them in summer."

Elias inhaled sharply, and when she tilted her chin to look up at him, he seemed frozen, staring at the flickering green ribbon. "This is a good omen," he said.

She returned her attention to the display, which was already fading. "You think so?"

"Yes." He tightened his arms around her almost possessively, but she found she didn't mind. In fact, she was surprisingly content, probably because she was warm, her belly was full, and she wasn't alone.

She kept her eyes on the sky where the aurora had been. "I always imagined the northern lights had magical power."

"They do," he said with sincerity. "The Native people believe the lights are the spirits of the animals they hunt. Those spirits can visit you, given the right circumstances."

Boat captains could be a superstitious lot, but even so, she was glad he hadn't poo-poohed her comment. Slowly, her eyes drifted closed, comforted by the steady beat of his heart against her cheek.

She woke in darkness to find herself cocooned in his arms, his front pressed along her back, his arm serving her as a pillow. The hard ground was digging into her hip, and she needed to adjust but didn't want to wake him. She shifted enough to ease the pain, then stared at the faint glowing coals of the fire. She should build it back up, but it was warm beneath the fur, and there wouldn't be many boats perusing the water in the dark, anyway. *I'll move in a minute*, she told herself, watching the horizon.

At her back, Elias inhaled deeply and nuzzled into her hair. She smiled to herself, imagining how embarrassed he'd be if he knew he was holding her like a teddy bear. Then she noticed a hard line against her backside. *Ok, maybe not a teddy bear.*

She wasn't sure if she should be flattered or offended. Her body had its own ideas, however, responding with a flood of heat between her legs. *This is Elias Sobol*, she reminded herself, biting her cheek. But would it be so wrong to find pleasure and comfort in each other's arms? Who knew if they'd ever find their way off this island. Plus, she'd come to realize she didn't hate him anymore.

Tentatively, she arched her back, pressing her ass against his groin. His arm circling her waist tightened, and he flexed, grinding his hips against her backside. *Oh, that's a big one.* She drew in a sharp breath and stilled, waiting to see what would happen next. Maybe he was still sleeping and his body had just automatically responded. But his breathing had changed, become shallower and charged with tension. Her own chest rose and fell beneath the solid weight of his arm, and a tingling between her legs needed to be touched.

When the stillness stretched past endurance, she took a deep breath. She wanted him—or at least, wanted sex. And his body seemed ready to oblige. Wrapping her fingers around his wrist, she eased his hand from her waist and lowered it down between her legs. Breathlessly, she waited for his response.

He groaned low in her ear, fingers curling against her core, cupping her mound. At the same time, he thrust his hips against her backside, his breathing harsh.

God, that feels so good. She whimpered and wriggled slightly, her own breathing down to shallow panting. Was she really doing this?

Twisting to look at his face, she found his eyes boring straight into her, the desire there unmistakable. She tilted her chin toward his face. At once, his mouth captured hers, his tongue caressing her lips as his fingers worked a gentle rhythm against her center.

A small moan escaped her, and she parted her lips, allowing his tongue full access. She slid a hand up his collarbone to touch the rough stubble along his jaw.

Without breaking the kiss, he propped himself on an elbow over her, kissing her deeply and passionately, a kiss like she'd never experienced before. Her head swam as if she'd been drinking. She rolled her knees toward him, opening her legs to his touch as he massaged over her jeans. It wasn't enough.

With her free hand, she opened her fly.

His hand delved inside before she'd finished lowering the zipper, sliding beneath her panties to her heated folds. One long finger slid along her slippery cleft, gliding over her lower lips with a slow and purposeful thrust that had her arching up to meet him.

"Lana," he said against her lips, then ravaged her mouth with kisses once more as his finger parted her and found her sensitive nub.

Shivers raced through her core, making her legs tremble and her nipples harden to aching peaks. She fumbled for his crotch, but his arm was in the way, and the sensations rolling through her were clouding her thoughts. She flexed upward to meet the increasing rhythm of his hand, rockets of pleasure building between her legs.

He dipped his finger into her channel, once, twice, three times, deeper with each thrust. She moaned, on the verge of climax, and realized she was whimpering against his kisses. The onslaught of desire was almost too much to bear. He plunged deep inside her, applying pressure in exactly the right place.

She exploded, crying out and arching her back as spasming waves of ecstasy rippled through her. Her legs shook, her insides contracted, and relief washed over her in consuming waves. She'd had no idea she'd needed release so badly.

His rhythm slowed, the pressure easing as he let her ride her orgasm to the very end. She lay limp against the ground, fighting to keep her eyes open. Elias was still looking into her face, and she expected him to yank her pants off and have his way. Wanted him to. She reached for the raincoat around his waist, but he turned her onto her side and lay down behind her, pulling her backside toward him once more. His erection still throbbed against her ass.

"You don't want to be with me?" she managed to croak out.

"It's okay," he said, confusing the shit out of her.

Did he not want her? Had she basically just forced herself on him, and he'd obliged out of pity? Her cheeks burned and her eyes misted with tears. At least the darkness hid her embarrassment—for now. Squeezing her eyes tightly closed, she pretended to sleep, wondering how the hell she would ever face him in the morning.

CHAPTER TEN

*E*lias wanted to bury himself inside Lana more than he'd ever imagined wanting anything in his life. His inner seal railed against his control, and his balls felt like they were going to explode. But he didn't trust himself to take her without claiming her. She wouldn't understand the bite, let alone forgive him if he forged a bond without her consent. He'd come so far in gaining her trust, he didn't want to risk alienating her again.

So instead of fucking her silly, he waited until her breathing steadied, her body stilled in sleep, then slipped from the pocket of warmth and walked down to the water. He needed to go for a swim to cool off. The tide was on its way back in, its inevitable regularity calming him. Without his pelt, he couldn't shift to his seal, but his human form was a strong swimmer. He waded in, letting the frigid water buffet his legs and hips before submerging completely.

Lying on his back in the current, he watched the sky lighten from midnight purple to patchy gray, and sent a silent prayer to the north where they'd seen the aurora, asking for guidance. The rare show had been a sign, he was certain of it. The lights were the source of shifter spirit animals, and they wanted Lana to join them—to become his mate.

Jacob's words back on the boat came to his mind. *Our ancestors would have whisked her off to a secluded island and had their way with her.* And here he was, alone on a secluded island with only his mate for company. Perhaps the gods were trying to tell him something. His crew had been right to send him back here.

Fuck, she'd been wet and willing, and he'd pushed her away. Why was he denying himself? There was no longer a husband to get in the way, and once he claimed her, she'd know without a doubt they were meant to be together. She might be freaked out by his selkie, but she wouldn't be able to deny the bond, and wasn't that what really mattered?

Hurrying back down a small trail to the beach, he returned to the small campsite. Lana lay on her side under the fur, wisps of her silky brown hair fluttering across her cheek. She was so damned beautiful it made his chest ache.

As he slid in beside her, she stiffened and twisted her head to look at him. "You're freezing!"

"Oh, sorry." He grimaced sheepishly.

She frowned, gaze raking his hair. "Why are you wet?"

"I went for a swim. It helps me think."

Her eyes widened, then she wriggled out from under the sealskin. "I'll let you warm up, then."

He grabbed her wrist lightly, "Stay, I'll warm up in a minute. You can help."

She pulled away. "I don't need your pity."

He gaped at her. Things had taken a left turn, and he blinked in confusion. "Why would you think I pity you?"

She tilted her head and narrowed her eyes. She had a smudge of dirt over one eyebrow and her cheeks were flushed. "Why else would you turn me down? It's fucking embarrassing."

The blood drained from his face as he realized she was talking about how he'd ended the make-out session earlier. "I stopped because I respect you."

She sneered and turned away. "It's fine. I do understand. We're enemies—"

He sat up and grabbed her shoulders, pulling her back to face him. "We're not enemies."

"Then what?" She scowled. "I've seen you leaving with all sorts of women at the bar. Don't tell me you haven't been intimate with them. It's obviously just me you don't want."

He couldn't let her think that, couldn't let her slip away like she had every time he'd come near her on the mainland. Without speaking, he leaned in and kissed her.

Her body trembled against him, then she melted into the kiss, one hand stroking his stubbled cheek. Gods, she was like nectar, and he plunged his tongue into her mouth, tasting her sweetness. After long moments, she broke the kiss and nibbled along his jawline to his ear. Her breath was husky as she murmured, "I'm on birth control and the doctor gave me a clean bill of health."

He nuzzled her ear in return, nipping the lobe. "I need you to know something first."

"What?" Her breath caressed his cheek as she dropped her head back to expose her neck and shoulder.

His seal about lost it then and there. *She's offering herself! Claim her now!*

He closed his eyes, panting as he brushed his mouth right over the spot where he would bite her and mark her as his forever. His teeth had sharpened, his selkie canines coming out with his growing desire, but he needed to slow down. She was human and wouldn't understand.

She trailed her fingertips over his chest and tweaked a nipple, then dipped her hand lower to the edge of the raincoat at his waist. He grabbed her wrist, stopping her exploration, and groaned, "I want you more than anyone I've ever met. You're different. Special. I never want you to look back and think I lied to you or took advantage of you."

"I wouldn't think that. I promise." She tugged against his grasp and sat upright to pepper his mouth with small kisses.

She didn't know what she was promising. This wouldn't be a one night stand. If he took her, he would take her completely. He couldn't let there be any misunderstanding between them. It was time for him to show her who he really was. To make her understand what she meant to him. But how did he go about telling her he wasn't human? "I'm not like other men."

"What do you mean?"

"I—" he cleared his throat. "I'm not human."

Wariness flashed over her face. "Okaaayy."

Great, now she thinks I'm crazy. Standing, he backed toward the lapping waves. "Please don't freak out. I have something I need to show you."

Before he could second guess himself, he tugged off the raincoat, pulling the sealskin up over his shoulders and willing the shift to take hold.

Lana drew her knees against her chest and gaped as Elias's body shimmered and he dropped to the ground. *What the hell is going on?* His skin transformed into silver fur, his face lengthened, and his arms transformed, flattening and spreading. A huge seal now posed on the beach in front of her, a scar bisecting one whiskery eyebrow. He had to weigh at least two hundred pounds, muscular shoulders and neck tapering to a pointed muzzle.

No way had that just happened. Men did not transform into animals.

Her heart threatened to break out of her chest. "What the hell!"

The seal lowered his head, liquid black eyes regarding her. Familiar eyes. *Elias's eyes.*

"Elias?" she breathed, back pressed tightly against the big driftwood log backing their campsite.

The creature nodded slowly.

She had to be dreaming. Hallucinating. Maybe this entire experience of being trapped on an island with her worst enemy—a very hot enemy—was a figment of her imagination. She looked around, trying to find something to confirm this was all a dream, but everything was so consistent. *So real.* From the crackling fire to the slight crunch of sand underneath the seal's flippers. "I must be going crazy."

The seal shimmered again, and once more Elias stood in front of her, dressed in nothing but a sealskin circling his hips. "You're not crazy. I'm a selkie."

She frowned, not familiar with that word. "Soooo... a man who can turn into a seal or the other way around?"

He laughed. "I spend most of my time as a man. But there are shifters who prefer their animal forms."

Shifter. That term she'd encountered in movies and books, but never in a million years imagined such a thing could be real. Elias had changed into a wild animal right here before her eyes. "You're the seal who saved me in the water. That's how you ended up here with me."

He nodded.

She stared at the fur covering his lower half. "Is your sealskin vest what gives you the ability?"

"Sort of. It's a part of me. Losing it would be worse than losing a limb."

In the years she'd known him, she couldn't recall seeing him without it. *Except for when he loaned it to you.* She frowned and lifted her eyes from the fur to meet his gaze. "But you took it off. You let me use it."

He hesitated, as if uncertain what to say next. Speaking so low she almost couldn't hear him, he said, "Yes. I would never leave it with anyone but you."

"Me?" Her insides quivered in response to the intensity of his dark gaze, but she refused to look away. Something important was happening here. "Why?"

"Because you're my mate."

"I'm your what now?"

"We're fated to be together." He stepped forward and knelt next to the fire. "It's a shifter thing."

A shifter thing. Part of her balked at the idea. Part of her was intrigued by it. "But I'm not a shifter. And earlier, you didn't want to..." She flushed, remembering his mouth against hers, his fingers beneath her panties. "Shouldn't you *want* to be with me if I'm your mate?"

"Oh, I do. Believe me, I do. But there will be consequences once we are together."

She gulped. "What kind of consequences?"

"If I take you, I'll claim you. I'll bind us together for the rest of our lives. And considering how you feel about me..."

He let the words hang there as she continued to stare at him. "I don't understand. All we've ever done is fight."

"My seal wanted you the first night we met. The moment I walked into that bar."

Understanding flooded her. "That's why you attacked Peter."

He rubbed the back of his neck, looking sheepish. "Attacked is a strong word."

She couldn't help but smile. For better or worse, she'd always been attracted to a man who defended what he thought was his. *Elias thinks you're his.* Strangely, the idea thrilled her. And it explained why she'd felt awkward every time she'd looked up to find him staring at her over the last few years. Every word he'd spoken, every glance she'd interpreted as malicious, now had a different meaning in her mind.

She covered her face with her hands and let out a lengthy breath. "I'm still not entirely sure this is real. I need some time to process."

"Of course." His soft, husky voice felt like it raised the temperature ten degrees. "But I think deep down you want me, too."

She squinted through her fingers, her brain hurting. Freaky as all this was, she couldn't deny she was attracted to this man. And how cool would it be to be able to swim like a seal? *He says it's fate.* More than once, now, fate had put her life in danger. And fate had allowed Elias to save her. Perhaps she should listen.

Reaching forward, she took his hand, enjoying the way his calloused fingers curled around hers in response. "So, where do we go from here?"

CHAPTER ELEVEN

*E*lias meant to take things slow, to woo Lana with stories about his family, his life. He'd planned to stroke her and soothe her and ease her into this decision. To have her full consent to not just sex, but everything he offered. But Lana was already aroused. He could smell it. He leaned forward toward where she sat with her back against the log until her breath fanned his face. More of her luscious arousal flooded the air, and her fingers tightened around his. *Damn taking it slow.*

He seized her mouth in a kiss.

Velvet soft, she parted her lips, raising her hands to his stubbled jaw. He reveled in her taste, her touch, her breath mingling with his, plunging into her sweetness, loving the way she parried her tongue against his in return. He slid one hand beneath the hem of her hoodie to glide along her silken skin.

She gasped at the contact, and her hands dropped from his face to pull off her hoodie. She struggled a moment to work it over her chin, and he took the opportunity to gaze at her pale pink skin, the taut peaks of her nipples jutting against her bra's thin red lace, the indentation above her collarbone where he'd place his claiming mark. His mouth watered at the sight.

Then she tossed the shirts aside and reached for him again, and he just about lost his mind.

He slipped one hand around her and deftly unclasped the bra. Sliding a thumb under the band, he lifted the fabric away, cupping his palm over her naked breast, her smooth, pillowy soft skin a perfect handful. "I've dreamed of doing this for so long," he said, reaching greedily for both mounds, kneading them under his palms.

She moaned and groped at his waist, fingertips digging beneath the sealskin. "I want to touch you."

He was happy to oblige. Yanking the pelt free, he spread the fur on the sand beside them. When he turned back, her attention was on his crotch, eyes wide and mouth slightly open. He reached down and circled his shaft. "Do you want this?"

Her throat moved in a swallow. "You're huge."

"I won't hurt you, I promise." He coaxed her to lay back against his fur. Although he burned to yank her jeans off and pound into her, he knew he needed to go slow. Women had told him he was big in the past, but he'd never hurt anyone, and he definitely didn't want to start now.

Placing one knee between hers, he licked a languid trail up from her belly button to the underside of one breast. Her skin twitched beneath his touch, and she let out a soft moan. In tightening circles, he lapped one breast with his tongue until he reached the nipple, loving the way it puckered in response. He rolled his tongue around the hard bud, then drew her in and sucked.

She cried out, arching upward to meet him, and he massaged her opposite breast, pinching and rolling the nipple into a matching peak. Clutching his shoulders, she writhed underneath him, hips rolling and back arching. Her heated center bucked against his thigh, slick with need. The woman was driving him wild, making his balls ache.

Mouth still on her nipple, he opened her fly. Her hands fumbled down to assist, and she edged the waistband off her hips, lifting her ass to shimmy the denim down her legs. Her cotton panties got carried along for the ride, exposing her triangle of dark hair. Her sweet arousal met his nose like ambrosia. His teeth sharpened as his seal rose to the surface, urging him to hurry up. To mount her, claim her. Gods, he needed her.

He left her breasts, kissing his way down her belly and breathing deeply. Parting her thighs with both hands, he licked up the inside of one, then the other, before planting his mouth against her folds.

She gasped and bucked. She was swollen and wet, and he plunged his tongue into her, lapping up her sweetness. He circled her clit until it pulsed under his tongue, nipping and sucking until she was panting with need.

"Please!" she begged, both hands knotted in his hair as she rocked her hips upward in time to his rhythm.

Grinning, he slid a long finger into her channel. She whimpered with pleasure, rising to meet him. Pumping his finger in and out in time to his tongue, he searched for the spot deep inside that would send her over the edge. He knew he'd found it when her muscles clamped around him. *So tight*. She cried out, shuddering and pulsing. He continued pumping until her climax reached its crest.

Then, before she could relax, he added a second finger, upping his pace as he curled against her g-spot.

She screamed his name, every muscle in her body tightening. Her legs shuddered. Her back arched. Wetness drenched his hand and pooled on the sealskin beneath her ass. As her orgasm subsided, he let out a satisfied growl.

She slumped limply against the fur, her quick breathing punctuated by tiny moans. "Oh my God. Oh, my God."

Pulling his fingers free, he gave a final, gentle lick to her swollen folds and let his gaze roam up her body to her flushed face. She glowed with passion, eyes dark as they met his. Her small pink tongue flicked out over her lower lip. Her scent coated his face, filled his nostrils, made his cock ache to feel her heat.

She opened her arms, her voice a husky whisper, "I want to feel you."

That was the only encouragement he needed. Positioning himself between her thighs, he feathered kisses up her belly until he nuzzled his face into the crook of her neck. This was where he would make his claim. Where he would place the bite that would bind them as mates forever. Her arms wrapped around his ribcage, and she lifted her legs over his hips as she turned and nibbled his earlobe.

He grasped his shaft, adjusting it until her wet folds kissed the head. His balls tightened with need. Much as he wanted to take her in one swift stroke, much as he'd prepared her, she still needed to adjust to him. He eased forward an inch.

She gasped, her exquisitely tight heat pulsing around him.

"Just relax, Lana," he murmured in her ear. He eased out, then back in, deeper this time, making shallow strokes as he stretched her, filled her. At last, his cock was fully encased in the heat of her pussy. "So good," he breathed against her ear.

Wriggling her hips under him, she said, "Fuck me, Elias."

"This is more than a fuck, baby." He pulled back and entered her again, seating himself hard against her hips, lingering, then doing it all over again. "This makes you mine."

He began pistoning into her, reveling in the little pleasure-noises Lana made as she met his thrusts. Her nails dug into his shoulders, and the pressure inside him built. His canines lengthened, his seal rising to the surface. *Claim her.* But he refused to let his seal take over this moment. This was more than instinct. This was something the human part of him had waited for his entire life. He wanted more than a mate. He wanted a lover. A partner.

He adjusted his angle, rolling his hips to make contact against her clit with each thrust. Gods, she was sexy. Her skin was slick with sweat, her nipples hard pebbles against his chest.

She tossed her head from side to side, moaning, "Oh, God. I'm coming again!" Her words rose to a scream as her heels dug into his backside, inner walls tightening around him with exquisite pressure.

Unable to restrain himself any longer, he pumped hard and deep, once, twice, and his seed erupted from him in a heated rush. At the same time, he bit down on her shoulder hard enough to taste the salty hint of blood. *Mine*, his seal thought with satisfaction.

Lana went limp, panting for breath beneath him. His entire body thrummed with pleasure, and he nuzzled into the crook of her neck, breathing deeply of her slight cinnamon mixed with his own scent. This is what the Bible meant by "of one flesh." He couldn't believe it had finally happened. Lana was his, now and forever.

CHAPTER TWELVE

*L*ana could barely catch her breath. She feathered her fingers along Elias's back, loving the way he covered her, warmed her, made her feel safe and exhilarated at the same time. She'd never had multiple orgasms before, and her entire body felt wonderfully wrung out. "That was amazing."

"It was everything I hoped for," Elias whispered and pressed a kiss onto her shoulder.

She frowned, remembering the feel of his teeth pricking her skin. "Did you bite me?"

"Yes," he murmured against her earlobe. "That's how mates claim one another."

Her heartbeat stuttered as she remembered he wasn't exactly human. He was a selkie, a *seal*. Animals weren't always very considerate during mating. She'd always been impulsive, but this time she might've let her hormones take things too far. "You should have warned me about that part."

"I'm sorry." He pulled back to peer into her face. "I took it for granted you would know. But the bite is already healed. Feel it."

She ran her fingers lightly over her shoulder, expecting fresh blood, but the pinprick wounds had already scabbed over. "That's weird."

"You'll heal faster now." His voice was full of pride.

"So can I change into a selkie now, too?"

A smile tugged his lips. "You would make an adorable seal. But no, there's more to it if you want to get an animal of your own." He rolled over, pulling her against his chest. "Now that we're mated, I can take you to the glacier where our magic originated. When the northern lights are active, a cave will open up, and if a mated human drinks from the water inside, they'll gain a spirit animal."

She relaxed against his chest, glad for the warmth he radiated in the brisk morning air. "Is that how you became a selkie?"

"No, I was born to a selkie family. Mating with a human is rare."

"Your parents are both selkies?" She sat up and looked at him, one hand still on his hard chest. "How many of you are there?"

"I have two brothers, and a small clan. Plus, there are other kinds of shifters, too. Wolves and bears are the most common, but there's a large raven clan up north, some eagles, even a few moose." Elias listed them off as if this was the most natural conversation in the world.

Imagining shifters around every corner, she frowned. "Do they all live in Kenai?"

"No, but you have met others." He licked his lips and folded his hand around hers, never breaking their gaze. "Your cousin is a wolf shifter."

Lana blinked, unable to process what he'd just said. "Ashlyn?" She shook her head briskly. "No fucking way. She would've told me!"

"It's true. Her mate, Kepler, is a wolf, too."

She gasped, all the weird shit that happened last summer clicking into place. "That's what happened when she was sick and had to close the bakery last summer. She got turned into a shifter. Wait, am I going to get sick?"

"No, there isn't usually sickness involved." He rubbed her arm in reassurance. "Your cousin was a special case. I only know her by reputation, but my understanding is that she saved the shifter community from a witch's curse."

Lana flopped back against the sand, her mind awash. "The family thought she was pregnant or something because she got married so fast." A light drizzle had started. "Shit! And that explains the dog hair on her couch!"

Elias chuckled. "Some of that might be from a bear. She and Kepler are the Alphas of a rather unorthodox pack."

"A p-pack?" Lana's stomach clenched at that thought. She sat up again and grabbed her hoodie, pulling it over hear head. *Oh my God. Is Cal a shifter, too?* He'd only started hanging around after Ashlyn got together with Kepler. And she'd slept with him. "Do you know Cal Bennett? Is he, um, one of you, too?"

"Yes." The jealous ferocity in Elias's voice made her heart race, reminiscent of her many arguments with Peter. The last thing she needed was to be trapped on this island with an angry man who could turn into an animal at will.

She tugged on her jeans and looked up at the sky, changing topics. "We should go back to the shelter until the weather clears. We can't keep a fire going in the rain."

Elias let out a long, measured breath. "I'm sorry. I can't help being jealous."

Lana didn't want to delve into this subject, so she simply nodded and hurried back to the spruce tree. She scooted inside and put her back to the trunk as he ducked in after her. Gripping his sealskin in one fist and her raincoat in the other, he knelt facing her, and her mouth went dry at the sight of his naked body. Between his muscular thighs, his half-rigid cock nestled in a small patch of silver hair that trailed up his rock hard abs to his navel. As she watched, his shaft seemed to swell. Could he be ready again so soon? Her gaze lifted to meet his.

He was smirking at her. "You put your clothes back on too soon."

Her body tingled with desire. She liked this new relationship feeling, but she knew it wouldn't last. She'd already seen what was to come when she'd brought up Cal. Right now, however, there was no one else around, so she might as well just enjoy the ride.

Slowly, she unbuttoned her jeans, watching his face as he focused on her hands. In a sudden move, he was on her, tugging her jeans off her legs. The moss and needles covering the ground were a decent cushion when she was wearing clothes, but a distraction sticking to her bare skin. She reached for the sealskin. "Give me that."

Rolling to one side, she spread it under them. The fur wasn't exactly soft, but it was warm and plush, as if his body heat still infused it.

He grabbed her ankles and pulled her toward him. "I like seeing you on my pelt."

With only her bottom half bare, she felt strangely exposed, more than if they'd both been naked. Without leaving her skin, his hands moved from her ankles up her knees, palms massaging her inner thighs. When his fingers reached her sex, he brushed his thumbs in slow, erotic circles over her lower lips.

She panted, watching him beneath hooded lids to see what he would do next. His attention fully between her parted legs, he continued massaging. He avoided delving between her folds, but her wetness lubricated his massage in a frustratingly arousing way until she was breathing hard and flexing upward, yearning for more.

Reaching down, she grabbed one of his wrists, trying to move his hand to her center. "Elias, please."

He let her push his thumb into her opening, but he only dipped once, then drew out and up in a firm line over her clit.

She jerked at the sensation and let out a gasp. "Oh, you tease."

He grinned, eyes full of hunger, and returned his thumb to her clit, circling it. Around and around he went, dipping lightly into her channel at an erratic pace until her legs stiffened and she shuddered with micro orgasms. She scooted her bottom toward him, riding against his hard thighs as she lifted herself, seeking his cock.

He sat back, pulling the object of her desire out of reach. "Turn around."

She obliged, lifting her ass in the air and pressing her cheek against the sealskin. It smelled like musk and fresh pine.

His hands settled onto her hips, and she felt his heat behind her. Her pussy clenched in anticipation. The broad, smooth head of his shaft rubbed up between her folds only once before he sank slowly into her. She pressed backward against him, wanting to take every millimeter he offered.

In slow, even strokes he began to pump, hands gripping her hips. As the pressure built, he seemed to swell inside her, filling her to capacity. Her pussy convulsed as her orgasm rose, but he didn't stop. He reached down and gripped the back of her neck, picking up his pace until he was ramming into her with a furious pace, balls slapping against her clit, hips against her backside as unyielding as a brick wall. She gasped as her initial orgasm crested into a second, stronger climax.

She clawed the fur, a scream ripped from her throat. At the same moment, Elias roared, sinking impossibly deep and holding himself there, filling her with liquid, pulsing heat.

He collapsed on top of her, and they both lay there together, panting. Despite the chill weather, Lana was sweating. She could never remember her pussy being this tired in her life, but it was exquisite.

Elias rolled off her, chest heaving and eyes closed. For a moment, she thought he'd abandoned her to sleep, but then he flung an arm out and tugged her toward him. "C'mere."

She giggled and moved over to lay against his chest. "You sound drunk."

"I am. Drunk on you." He opened his eyes and turned to look at her. "Gods, woman, you are breathtaking."

She sighed in contentment and played her fingers along the definition of his rock-hard pecs. "You didn't bite me this time."

"Did you want me to?"

"No, I just didn't know if that would be a thing every time."

"The first was the most important." He tightened his arm around her. "You're mine forever now, no matter what."

She closed her eyes, too tired to think as she let his breathing lull her to sleep.

CHAPTER THIRTEEN

*E*lias had never in his life expected to feel as much joy as he did over the next two days. He brought Lana fish, and she scavenged clams and small crabs for them. The rain made it unpleasant to stay on the beach, but they were plenty warm together in their bower beneath the spruce tree. He knew he should go summon help and get her back to Kenai, but Lana never suggested it, and the selfish part of him wanted to keep her all to himself a while longer.

They sat cross-legged on his pelt beneath the tree, the stringent scent of sap filling the area. Lana was putting the finishing touches on a heart she'd carved into the trunk of the tree.

"Ugh, that was dumb. This will never come off." She rubbed at the sticky splotches darkening her fingers.

"But I bet no one has ever made love on this island before. We're the first and only."

He took her hand and kissed it, smiling at her with adoration. "This will always be our special spot."

She smiled back, a matching glow in her eyes.

"Are you hungry?" he asked. "I can go catch fish."

"Any chance you could catch me a jelly doughnut?"

He laughed. "Sorry. And I don't recommend the jellyfish around here."

She pursed her mouth thoughtfully. "Ashlyn tries to give all her pastries Alaskan names. I should suggest jellyfish doughnuts."

"Jellyfish doughnuts might not sound very appealing to most Americans."

"What do you mean? It's adorable! Cute little fishies filled with raspberry jelly."

"Won't people think that looks like blood?"

She bit her lip. "Oh, I didn't think of that. But now I want a doughnut more than ever. I need to stop talking about pastries." She covered her eyes with one arm. "Tell me more about your childhood. You said your mom wasn't around, but if mates are so important to shifters, why'd she leave?"

His mood soured. He hated thinking about his mom, let alone talking about her. But Lana was his mate. She should know everything about him.

"Many shifters marry, have families, and live perfectly contented lives without meeting their mate. We don't expect to. But when we do, the bond we form is, well, I guess you could call it unbreakable. And undeniable." He shifted uncomfortably, and when he spoke again, his voice was a raspy whisper. "My mom and dad had been together almost fifteen years when she met her mate."

Lana flung her arm aside and frowned at him. "You mean your dad wasn't her mate?"

"No." He shook his head slowly. "She loved my dad and hated hurting him, but she met her mate during a shopping trip in Anchorage, and that was that. She lives with him in Seattle now."

Her mouth formed a shocked circle. "How could she abandon her kids like that?"

Elias shrugged. "She wanted to take us with her, but my brothers and I decided we couldn't do that to Dad. She had someone. Dad only had us." He sighed. "Problem was, he loved her, even though they weren't mates. Loved her hard enough to let her go, he always said. But it broke something inside him. He's a good man. I hated her for a long time." Even now, his feelings about her were mixed. Lana had made him realize how intense the mating bond could be, but a mother's bond to her children was supposed to be just as strong, and she'd left them. Rejected him and his brothers and never looked back.

"Did your dad find his own mate, then?"

"No. Most shifters never find their true mate. You're special. Rare."

"I don't care what excuse she gave, she had a responsibility." Lana shook her head. "Kids need their mom. She should never have moved away like that."

He smiled, thinking of Lana cradling their first child. "You'll make a great mother."

"Maybe someday," she said, averting her eyes. "Tell me about how you grew up. Could you change into a seal right away? I bet that's a challenge for shifter parents."

He lay back on the pelt next to her and put his hands behind his head. "Most kids don't gain the ability to shift until puberty. I learned when I was fourteen."

"Oh, that makes sense." Lana yawned, turning to face him. "How will it work when I get a seal? Do I just know how to become one automatically?"

He grimaced. "I forgot to mention something. You may not get a seal. The spirits could give you a different animal. Or no animal at all."

"You said we'd visit the glacier, and I'd get a spirit seal."

"I said a spirit animal. And it is all up to whatever magic gives us our power."

She made a frustrated noise. "I'll probably end up being a herring shifter or something."

He tweaked her nose. "More like a killer whale. You're too bold to be a herring."

Her eyes glinted. "Are there orca shifters?"

"I've only heard of one, and it may be nothing but rumor. I think whales are intelligent in their own right, more than most of the animals we share our souls with." His seal balked at the insult, but he calmed it by sliding a hand under Lana's shirt, her silky skin warm. Her full breast filled his palm, nipple hardening as he gently pinched it.

She closed her eyes and ran her tongue along her bottom lip. "Elias Sobol, you are going to be the death of me."

Pushing her shirt all the way up, he leaned over and took the nipple in his mouth. He could sense their time here winding down, and he was going to make the most of it.

Lana had no strength left. Not a single ounce. It was as if Elias's touch was a drug, and she was an addict. All it took was a glance, and she wanted to melt, and she could barely focus on anything but how he made her feel when he caressed her body. She'd lost count of the number of orgasms she'd had since this all began, but she was pretty sure it was more than her lifetime in total. Apparently selkies were sex machines.

Still breathing hard from their last encounter, she lay limply against the fur, staring at the boughs overhead. She was still thinking about his family, feeling lucky her parents had always been solid. "Hey, is your mom the reason you didn't try to break up my marriage?"

"Yes. But now that you're free, I'll apply for a marriage license the moment we get back to Kenai. Do you want a church wedding or something less formal?"

"Whoa, slow down." She threw up both hands, panic rising inside her. This was starting to sound way more serious than she first imagined. "I thought this mate thing was just physical. You didn't say anything about getting married."

She and Peter had only dated a few weeks before they got married. She'd been enamored of him and his rough fishing life. Mom had tried to warn her not to move so fast, but Lana always seemed to act first and think later. Not long after the wedding, Peter grew suspicious of everything and everyone. He'd even fired his deckhand, jealous of the way she joked with him. Elias was a brawler, just like Peter had been. The last thing she needed was another man telling her where she could go or what she could do.

"Don't you want a ceremony for your human family?" he asked. "For our honeymoon, we can stay at Paxon Lodge. It's run by a clan of ravens not far from the glacier. They cater to the newlywed shifter crowd."

"I think you got the wrong idea here. I'm not marrying you." She was not about to tie herself to another man legally, financially, or even socially. "You said this was a shifter thing. A physical thing. Let's keep it that way."

"Lana, I'm sorry. I'm terrible at romance. Once we get back to Kenai, I promise to court you properly."

"No." She fumbled to pull her panties free of the inside-out legs of her jeans. "I promised myself I'd never marry again after Peter."

"Why not? We're *mates*," he said in a growly voice.

Lana didn't meet his gaze as she slid her panties on. Her nether regions were still sensitized from their intense lovemaking, and she couldn't deny she wanted more, especially when he used that growly voice of his. *It's only chemistry*. Physically, they were incredibly compatible; she could well believe no other lover would ever compare. But that didn't mean she would marry him. "Animals mate all the time. I had no idea you meant you wanted marriage."

"You are the most frustrating female I have ever encountered." He yanked his sealskin up over his hips. "What did you think I was doing when I claimed you?"

"Hell if I know! I thought it was a turn on for your seal or something. You didn't even warn me you would bite me." She rose, shimmying her legs into her sandy jeans. "Let's just focus on getting off this island, all right?"

"About that." Elias adjusted the fur around his hips. "It's best if no one knows I'm with you."

"Why?"

He shrugged. "No one knows that I'm missing."

"Your crew doesn't know you're gone?" She straightened, raising her eyebrows at him.

"They know I'm with you. And they wouldn't report me missing."

She let out a slow breath, realizing what he meant. "They're shifters, too?" Then she realized something else. "What the hell, Elias? You mean you could've brought back help this entire time?"

CHAPTER FOURTEEN

*E*lias felt heat climb up his chest and fill his face. This situation with Lana was getting more complicated by the minute, and it seemed she was just itching for a reason to hate him again. "Sure, I could've gone for help. But how would I have explained that to you? 'Oh, by the way, I'm going to disappear without a trace after saving you, but don't worry, I'll be fine.'"

Anger rolled off her in palpable waves. "Better than tricking me into having sex with you."

"Trick you? In no way did I trick you. You *begged* me to fuck you."

"I did no such thing!" Her cheeks flushed bright red.

He took a step closer, looking down into her face. "I gave you a chance to refuse. More than once. You wanted me as much as I wanted you."

"I just wanted some comfort! Something to take my mind off being stranded on a remote island." She swept a hand out to indicate the rocky bank. "Only it turns out I didn't need to be stranded if my knight in shining armor had any honor at all."

Heat flared deep inside his chest. "If I had no honor, I would've stolen you away from that no-good husband of yours years ago."

Her eyes glistened with unshed tears, and frustrated though he was, he did not want to make her cry. He softened his tone. "Listen, I did try to get help." He reached for her hands, but she jerked them away. "That first day, when you sprained your ankle and almost drowned again, that's where I'd gone."

She sneered. "You said you never wanted me to look back on this and think you lied to me, but you've been lying this entire time. If you went for help, why didn't you come back with it, huh? Why are we still here?"

"My mutinous crew insisted I use the opportunity to claim you."

She let out a bitter laugh. "Oh, you used the opportunity, all right."

"You don't understand. I had to prove to you that I'm not the enemy!" He grabbed her shoulders.

"Let go of me." She jerked herself free and shoved against his chest, backing away. "You are the enemy! You're a monster! You know that? I fucking hate you!"

Her words slammed into him like a harpoon. Blackness pressed at the edges of his vision, and he let out a slow breath. Lana was supposed to want to be with him now. To be unable to resist him. But the mating bond obviously hadn't changed her feelings. She would forever view him as the enemy.

Turning, he stalked toward the water, pulling his sealskin up until it covered him, and dove into the curling waves without a backward glance. He was done trying to prove he was worthy of her love.

Love is not important, his inner seal growled. *We claimed her. She's ours.*

He surfaced and took a breath, raw air burning his lungs. Perhaps the bond was physical only, as Lana had suggested. Perhaps hoping for love was asking too much. Mom had loved dad. She said it over and over, even as she was packing her bags. Had she ever said she loved her mate? He'd spent little time with her after the divorce, and he didn't know.

The smart thing to do right now—the honorable thing —was get her off the island. But the selkie side of him didn't want to let her go. For a fleeting moment, he wondered if he could keep her there forever, build a little house and ferry goods to her. *Of course not.* That would be insane. Keeping her prisoner would only make her hate him more, and someone would eventually find her. Besides, Lana deserved more than a crude life on a deserted island. His mate deserved the world.

Resigning himself to a life of watching her from a distance once more, he sent a mental signal to his crew, sensing them several miles to the east. He'd call the Coast Guard and tell them he'd spotted her signal fire, and they would take care of the rest.

He reached the *Utkin* and Bobby gave him a hand over the gunwale, his bearded face split by a leering grin. "So, do we have a new crew member?"

Elias gritted his teeth. "No." He'd assumed if he ever convinced Lana to mate with him, she'd join his crew, but now that he thought about it, he knew that had been a stupid idea right from the start. She had her own life. "She's the captain of her own boat and always will be."

"All right, all right." Bobby stepped back to give him room. "A new captain in our fleet, then. Two boats are better than one."

"Woo hoo, we're a fleet!" Dean cheered.

"We're not a fleet." Elias adjusted his sealskin around his hips and stalked toward the wheelhouse.

Jacob had been manning the helm, and now blocked the doorway, arms crossed over his chest. "We said you couldn't come back on board until you claimed her."

Elias bared his teeth. "Not that it's any of your business, but I did claim her. Now get out of my way."

Jacob didn't resist as Elias shoved him aside. Bobby pushed into the wheelhouse with the other men close behind. "You want us to lower the skiff to go pick her up?"

"No. Search and Rescue can take it from here."

"We can get to her faster—"

"I said no! Now get out." Elias put every ounce of Alpha into his command and thrust a finger back toward the open door.

Everyone backed out of the wheelhouse except Jacob, who stepped inside and closed the door behind him. It wasn't real privacy, since Elias was certain everyone could hear them from the other side, but at least they couldn't see how broken he was.

Jacob leveled him with a stare. "Tell me what's going on."

They'd been through plenty of tough times, and if Elias didn't explain things, his friend would likely toss him off the boat again. "She still hates me, all right?"

Jacob scrunched one eye doubtfully. "Did you, um… force her?"

"No!" Elias glowered at his friend. "No, I did not force her. You know me better than that. Physically, Lana and I are a perfect match. My seal is quite pleased with himself. But she thinks I lied to her. Plus, she still loves her husband."

"Isn't her husband dead?" Confusion twisted Jacob's features, mirroring Elias's own inner turmoil.

"Yeah." Elias's lips curled with self-loathing. *I can't even compete with the guy after he's dead.* How pathetic was he? He slumped into the pilot's chair and stared out the windows at the choppy water. "I should never have gone back to that island."

Jacob pulled a pair of sweatpants from a nearby cubby and tossed them at him. "Why don't you get your naked ass off that chair and dress like a normal human being. I'll bring you some coffee."

Coffee sounded great, but he couldn't help thinking about Lana, cold and alone on the island. Nasty weather was pressing in once more, rain blurring the view through the windshield. What if she did something stupid before Search and Rescue arrived?

The pit of his stomach ached. She had a tendency to let recklessness get the better of her. He snatched up the radio mike. "Coast Guard, this is the *Utkin*. We spotted what looks like a signal fire on an island nearby. We can't approach because of submerged rocks. Over."

"Roger that, *Utkin*. Send us your coordinates and we'll dispatch a helicopter. Thank you."

Well, that's that. Lana had made it clear she could handle herself. She would soon be back in the human world, anyway. Back to her old life. He shoved his legs into the sweatpants, reforming the shape of his sealskin into his usual long vest.

Jacob returned with a steaming mug of coffee, and Elias took a grateful sip, letting the hot liquid burn a trail down his throat. It was bitter and had been sitting on the burner too long, but it woke him up. He nodded at his friend. "Thank you."

"I'm sorry, man." Jacob sipped from his own mug. "If we'd known things would end like this, we wouldn't have forced the issue. Does she know you're a selkie?"

"Yes, she knows everything. Things were actually pretty good until I said I wanted to marry her." The boat took a wave sideways, tilting precariously until Elias adjusted their heading. "She doesn't want a life with me. Why did fate give me a woman who can never love me?"

"Maybe she just needs time. I mean, she literally despised you just last week."

Elias grimaced. "I think she despises me even more now." How was he going to face her every time they bumped into each other? "This is my mom and dad all over again."

Jacob frowned. "This is nothing like what happened between your parents."

"Different situation. Same story. Lana loves her husband, but she's mated to me." Elias slammed a fist against the arm of his chair and squeezed his eyes shut against the hopelessness.

"Lana's husband is *dead*, dude. Not hanging around to make her feel guilty."

Hands tightening into fists, Elias glared at his friend. "My dad was not *hanging around*. And he did not try to make Mom feel guilty. I'm moving the *Utkin* back to Homer as soon as the season's over. I can't stand to see her every day."

"Do you really believe you can walk away?"

"Well, I can't escape with her somewhere else. Her husband's ghost will follow us, it'll always be hanging around. It's best if I just let her go."

If Lana didn't want him, the best thing he could do was leave her alone to live her life.

CHAPTER FIFTEEN

*L*ana felt sick as she stared toward the empty gray horizon. The pain in Elias's eyes when she'd said she hated him had sobered her like a bucket of ice water, freezing her in place. Why had she said that? It wasn't true. Sure, she was confused, frustrated, and pissed as hell, but she didn't hate him.

But before she could apologize, he was gone, his sleek, dark seal form riding the waves before disappearing beneath the surface. Why was she so damned impulsive? It caused her no end of trouble. She understood why he'd held back the truth and knew she hadn't been tricked into sex. But the emotions he drew from her felt too raw to face, too real, too *permanent*. Until she got off this damned island, she couldn't trust her feelings about any of this.

Pulling her hoodie up around her head, she cinched the tie under her chin and added her raincoat over the top. She hadn't needed the extra warmth for days. The wind was picking up again, and without Elias's heat, a chill was sinking deep into her bones. Had he gone for help? She'd accused him of having no honor, but although his priorities may have been misguided, he'd taken care of her, kept her alive, told her the truth in the end. She had the feeling he'd swim to the North Pole for her if she asked him to. He was the most honorable person she'd ever met.

And she'd treated him horribly.

The fire struggled to remain burning, the damp logs hissing and steaming, and the wind kicked gusts of sand at her. Unsure what to do next, she gathered more driftwood and hunched down between the big log and the fire. She was exhausted, and her mind kept replaying scenes from the last few days. Elias's sultry grin when she'd first woken next to him under the spruce tree. How cute he'd been when he tried to dig out that giant hunk of driftwood. Their first kiss.

And the claiming.

Her fingers rubbed the spot on her shoulder where he'd bitten her. It didn't hurt. In fact, it tingled pleasantly as her fingers traced over it. She'd never felt so close to another person as she had during their joining. Without him here, the island felt barren, and so did her heart. What would it be like if she kept seeing him, not only here, but in Kenai? He'd promised to cook for her, and she imagined a candlelit dinner followed by a lazy soak in her hot tub underneath the stars. Did seals enjoy hot tubs? She pictured him in her bed, his lips hot against her neck as they tangled between smooth sheets...

The rhythmic thump of a helicopter cut through her thoughts. She shot to her feet, scouring the low-hanging clouds. Where was it? Frantically feeding the fire more sticks, she coaxed a hunk of driftwood into flames, hoping the pilot would see her signal.

As if it knew exactly where to look, the helicopter emerged from the clouds above the beach. She waved her arms, tears of relief rolling down her cheeks. "I'm here!"

The craft bobbed and swayed overhead, kicking sand and salt into her eyes. The tide was in, and there obviously wasn't enough room to land. Shielding her face in the crook of one arm, she backed up until she reached the sharp wall of rocks on the edge of the cove. The helicopter's side door opened, ejecting a man on a cable. He dropped to the ground and quickly detached the line. The cable swung wildly as the helicopter rose, rotors struggling to keep the craft steady in the gusting wind.

She rushed forward as the man yanked off his helmet, revealing a broad freckled face and reddish gold hair.

"Cal?" She gaped at the trooper as he crushed her to him, squeezing her breathless.

"Jesus, Lana. You're alive! Everyone was certain you drowned!"

She squeezed him back, uncaring that he'd been a prick to her in the past. He was here to save her. "I'm so relieved you found me."

Suddenly, he pushed her away, nostrils flaring as he frowned at her shoulder. "Are you alone here?"

Her breath caught, and her hand instinctively covered the spot where Elias had bitten her. *Cal is a wolf shifter.* Could he sense she'd mated with Elias? She laughed uncomfortably and glanced out over the water. A dark form surfaced several hundred yards from shore, then disappeared again. *Elias.* Of course he'd want to make sure the rescue team found her. But he'd said not to tell anyone he'd been on the island with her. Did that include other shifters? She had to assume so.

Turning a bright smile back toward Cal, she swept a hand to indicate the beach. "Nobody here but me."

His eyes narrowed, but he didn't press her. "All right," he said slowly. "Let's get you out of here. We need to hurry before this wind gets any worse."

From a small backpack, he pulled a harness and helped her step into it, tightening its straps around her thighs and chest. He spoke into a radio on his shoulder, then rubbed his fingers over his mouth. "Dammit. Pilot says using the line in this weather has become too dangerous. We're going to have to hunker down here a while longer."

The helicopter pivoted and sped north, the thumping sound of the rotor quickly swallowed by the roar of the wind. Lana stared after it in shock. "They're leaving?"

"Once the storm subsides, they'll be back."

This couldn't seriously be happening. First she was trapped here with Elias, who she'd hated, now she was alone with Cal, who she'd had an awkward one-night-stand with after her husband's death. It was almost funny. In fact, it *was* funny. A bubble of hysterical laughter swelled inside her chest. She wrapped her arms around herself and bent over, giggling.

"Sit down and drink this." Cal thrust a bottle of water between her numb fingers. "You're probably dehydrated."

Still choking on laughter, she sat with her back against the driftwood log. Cal removed a silvery space blanket from his pack and tried to spread it across her legs, but the wind ripped it loose and sent it hurtling down the beach. Swearing, he ran after it, catching it under a booted foot. He grabbed it in one fist and turned to hold it up triumphantly, plastic crackling fiercely as the wind tried to rip it from his grasp.

Out on the waves, the seal had moved closer to shore. As she watched, Elias shed his seal form and rose from the frothing surf like a silver deity. He stood submerged to his hips, silver fur receding from his chest back into the wrap around his hips. A wave crashed over his shoulders, but the man stood rock-solid against the onslaught, his face frozen into a dark scowl.

She stopped breathing as her mate walked out of the water, every inch of him built from unyielding muscle. She'd seen that look before on Peter. Jealousy. Aggression. *No, no no!* The last thing she wanted was these two men breaking into a brawl, not here, not anywhere. "Elias, stop! Go back."

Busy tucking the space blanket around her legs, Cal only glanced over his shoulder, then shot her a smug look. "I thought someone else was around." Seeing her expression, his pale eyebrows furrowed. "Did he hurt you?"

"No," she said quickly, unable to tear her eyes away from Elias. "He's... he's my mate."

Elias stopped a few paces away, hands balled into fists at his sides. "Do you need assistance?"

Cal tucked the space blanket under her feet and stood directly between them. The trooper put his hands on his hips—not quite a challenge, but definitely letting Elias know he wasn't afraid. "We'll be okay. The chopper will come back as soon as it can."

To Lana's surprise, Elias only nodded, sparing her a brief glance before stalking back to the water. He disappeared into the waves as steadily as he'd emerged.

Her adrenaline rush evaporated, and her death-grip on the water bottle eased. She felt as if she'd fallen overboard again, trying to keep her head above water with nothing to cling to. *What the hell just happened?* Elias hadn't started a fight. Hadn't insisted on staying to keep an eye on her, even though he was obviously jealous. He hadn't even said anything aggressive, just offered to help. She blinked in utter confusion.

Cal squatted down in front of her, his gaze concerned. "Did he force you into mating with him?"

"No!" she said again, guilt heating her as she remembered accusing Elias of just that. "I thought he was going to punch you, that's all."

"Ahhh," Cal said. "He knows about us, I take it?"

"Yes," she whispered. Elias knew, and he hadn't exploded into a jealous rage. He was nothing like Peter. Everything she'd assumed about him had been wrong. He respected her wishes. Allowed her room to breathe.

And she'd just let him walk away again without asking him to forgive her. Without telling him she was sorry. What was wrong with her?

"I wouldn't worry about it," Cal said flippantly. "It was ages ago, and you were a free woman at the time. You hungry?" He dug inside his pack.

She numbly accepted the energy bar he offered, only half listening as he described how search teams had been combing the area for days. *I fucked up*, kept repeating in her head. She'd made a lot of mistakes in her life, but this felt like the biggest one yet.

Elias watched Lana from far out on the waves. The wind had turned brutal, churning the water into massive swells, and his view of the shore disappeared and reappeared like a slideshow. Click, Cal handing Lana something. Click, a wall of gray water. Click, Lana stirring the fire. Click, water.

Jealousy formed a hard knot in his chest, weighing on him like an anchor. He turned out to sea several times, intending to leave Search and Rescue to do their job. But time and again, he circled back to the island instead.

Earlier, when he'd shown himself to Cal, he'd had an ulterior motive, and he wasn't proud of it; he'd wanted the other shifter to know Lana was his. It was petty, he knew, but he couldn't help it. Lana was alone with a man she'd been intimate with before, and the mate bond didn't seem to work on humans the same way it did on shifters. But Cal was a shifter, and he knew better than to touch another shifter's mate.

The waves grew rougher, and the tide shifted direction. A pod of belugas passed behind him in pursuit of salmon, their joyful chirps oblivious to the storm overhead. Then, between one wave and the next, Lana and Cal were gone. Fear clenched his heart. What if a wave had swept her out to sea?

He darted through the waves, pulling himself on land to find the campfire dead, blackened bits of wood spread across the beach by the waves. The grass clinging to the sand near shore lay battered into submission by the wind. He'd just opened his mouth to call out when his sensitive hearing detected voices inland.

Following the sound to the spruce tree where he and Lana had first sought shelter, he heard Cal's laughter roll from beneath the thick branches. The sharp odor of spruce sap reached him and the hair on the back of his neck rose. What would he do if he found her in the other shifter's arms?

His lip curled, and a low growl rose from his chest, ripped out to sea by the storm. Hands clenched into fists, he dropped to his knees, his seal urging him to crawl under the boughs and drag the other shifter off his mate. To bash his head in and tear him limb from limb.

Then Lana's sweet voice reached him. "Peter kept a stash of these on the boat."

His rage sucked back into his chest like a vortex pulling a ship to the ocean floor. It always came back to her dead husband. No matter what Elias thought of the man, she loved him and always would. She didn't want Elias.

But we claimed her, his seal insisted. *We love her.*

He sucked in a breath. Love? His seal didn't tend to think in human terms. Desire, lust, possessiveness, those were all familiar sensations. But love?

Her stubborn loyalty, her intelligence, even her frustratingly spontaneous choices filled him with joy and a desire to make her happy. His seal was right; he loved her.

And Lana hated him. Hated him so badly, she'd told him to go back to the water when he'd shown himself to Cal. It didn't matter that he'd done the right thing and summoned help. She didn't want him around, would probably never trust him again. He'd tainted any chance of showing her he was not the enemy, and now he had to live with it.

The best way he could love her was to let her go.

Hurrying back to the crashing waves, he shifted back into his seal and left the island. This was the hardest thing he'd ever done, but he would honor her wishes.

Diving beneath the waves, he followed the current out to sea. He would stop at the *Utkin* to tell his crew he would not be returning to Kenai.

From now on, he would live his life as a seal, alone on the open water.

CHAPTER SIXTEEN

*T*he helicopter returned as soon as the storm abated, and as it lifted her away from shore, relief filled Lana. But leaving things unresolved with Elias left her sick to her stomach. *You can track him down when you get back to Kenai,* she reminded herself as she watched the island disappear on the horizon.

But she hated waiting.

She sat back and tried to enjoy the helicopter ride. She'd never been in one before, and the way it dipped and swayed felt a lot like her boat. But the water passing by so far below made her woozy, and she finally had to stop looking out the window all together.

When the helicopter finally set down at the small airport, a flashing ambulance waited on the tarmac, and a crowd of onlookers had rallied outside the chain link fence near the gate. A pair of paramedics escorted her through the rain into the back of the ambulance to be checked out. She fidgeted as the female medic fixed a blood pressure cuff around her arm. Where was Ashlyn? Elias? She'd assumed someone would be here to greet her. Elias had almost an eight hour head start, surely he'd reached Kenai by now.

She shrugged off the medics' gloved hands. "I need to go."

"You're probably dehydrated. We should start an IV." The female paramedic gripped Lana's arm.

"No, I don't need it. I'm fine, really." She ripped off the blood pressure cuff, wanting to get out of this ambulance and go find her mate. They were meant to be together. She'd been a fool to deny it. She only hoped she wasn't too late to make things right.

"Stop being in such a rush," the male paramedic admonished, adding his hand to her other shoulder to prevent her from standing. "You've just been through a harrowing experience. You're allowed to take a moment to breathe."

Lana thrust away their hands and ducked out of the open double doors into the drizzling rain. She couldn't tell them the real reason she needed so desperately to go, so she said, "The fish are running. I can't afford to miss another opening."

"You're no good to anyone if you keel over from dehydration." The woman followed her out of the ambulance.

"It's been raining for five straight days. I'm not dehydrated."

At the fence, she spotted her cousin Ashlyn alongside Jeanette, raincoats pulled up over their heads and fingers threaded through the chain link. People snapped photos, and a local reporter started shouting questions as she rushed over. Ignoring everyone's stares, she put her hand over Ashlyn's on the wires. "Why didn't you come greet me?"

"Immediate family only on the tarmac." Ashlyn pressed her forehead to the fence, strands of pink hair plastered against her cheeks. "Are you okay?"

"Yes, I just need to get out of here." Lana headed toward the gate, paralleled by Ashlyn and Jeanette.

As they walked, Jeanette explained how the Coast Guard had to tow the *Willy Nilly* back to port. Lana hardly heard her as she scanned the small crowd. The ubiquitous raincoats made everyone look similar, but there was no sign of Elias.

"Have you seen the *Utkin* by chance?" Lana asked as she waited for the security officer to open the gate and let her out.

Jeanette frowned. "The *Utkin*? I think they're anchored in the river. Why?"

Thinking quickly, Lana said, "I heard they called in my location. I want to say thank you."

The moment she stepped through the gate, Ashlyn crushed her in a tearful hug. "Thank God you're all right. I thought you'd died."

Jeanette joined the hug. "I'm so sorry I let you fall overboard. I should've come on deck with you."

"So we could both be swept overboard?" Lana hugged both women back, fighting tears of her own. "Stop apologizing. None of this was your fault."

After a few minutes of describing how she'd survived on the island without mentioning anything about Elias, she gestured toward the eavesdropping reporter. "Can we go? I'll tell you more when we're not so public."

"Of course!" Ashlyn took her hand, leading her toward the parking lot.

Lana stopped at Jeanette's car, pulling her hand from her cousin's. "I'm going back to the *Willy Nilly* with Jeanette."

Her cousin narrowed her eyes and clamped Lana's wrist in a death grip. "No, you're not. You need to eat first. Come to the bakery with me and I'll make you a sandwich.

Then you can take care of the rest of your business." When Lana opened her mouth to argue, Ashlyn added, "Cal called me from the helicopter. We ned to talk."

"Oh." Lana recognized the determination in Ashlyn's gaze. Her cousin knew. She wasn't getting out of this until she'd explained everything. Turning a tight smile on Jeanette, she said, "I'll call the repair guy and have him look at the navigation wiring. Be there as soon as I can."

Jeanette nodded. "Good to have you back, Captain."

Lana slid into the front seat next to Ashlyn. As soon as they were on the road, Ashlyn asked, "Elias Sobol? Really? How did that happen? You hate him."

Lana felt her cheeks heat. "Yes."

"I can't believe it." Ashlyn shook her head. "You hate him!"

The word *hate* made Lana flinch. That was the last thing she'd said to Elias—to her mate—before he'd left. "I did hate him. But I don't anymore."

As Ashlyn drove, Lana explained everything that had happened as best as she could. "I didn't really mean it when I said he was a monster. But he wanted to get married, you know?"

Ashlyn pulled into the parking lot and cut the engine. "You're mad at him because he asked you to marry him?"

"He didn't ask. He assumed. And why do mates need to be married, anyway?" She followed Ashlyn through the back door to the bakery. Her stomach growled loudly as she was enveloped by the delectable aromas of fresh bread, vanilla, and butter.

"I think you're overreacting because you're comparing him to Peter." Ashlyn pulled two freshly baked hoagie rolls from the display case and started piling on oven-roasted turkey.

"But we hardly know each other. I can't go from hating him one week to marrying him the next. That's crazy. Besides, isn't mating just physical?"

"Kepler and I only knew each other a few days, but it was as if our souls recognized each other. He's my perfect match."

Lana thought about how empty she'd felt when Elias had walked away, how the pain on his face had seared a path directly through her heart. She'd always been too bold, too impulsive. It seemed she was always making wrong choices and trying to make the best of her regrets. Right now she couldn't decide if she wanted to go home and cry into her pillow or scream her love for

Elias from the rooftops. "Well, right now I feel like an emotional teenager again, but this time on steroids."

Ashlyn cracked a smile and handed her the sandwich. "The mating bond has a tendency to make you giddy one moment and angsty the next."

Lana accepted the sandwich and took a huge bite. The lettuce had just the right amount of crunch, and the turkey made her mouth water. "Thanks." She chewed a few minutes, thinking about Elias. "So I'm going to feel like this the rest of my life?"

"I can't speak for your relationship, but the highs and lows leveled out once Kepler and I decided to be together. I think you need to give Elias a chance."

"More like he needs to give me one. I really hurt him." She stared at the food in her hand, no longer hungry. "Can I borrow your car? I have to get back to the *Willy Nilly.*"

"Why don't you go freshen up, then I'll drive you. There are toiletries and a change of clothes in the bathroom cupboard you can borrow."

Lana gave her a grateful smile and went to wash up. She was hurt Elias hadn't come to meet her at the helicopter, but she didn't blame him after the way she'd acted. Besides, he'd missed the last two commercial openings because of her, and when the run was in, a fisherman stopped for nothing. *Except maybe saving a mate.*

Ashlyn drove her to the boat ramp where Jeanette met her with the zodiac. After dropping her crew mate back on the *Willy Nilly*, Lana headed toward the *Utkin* where it was anchored in the river. Bluegrass music floated from the deck, and her boat's inflated pontoon bumped alongside for several minutes without anyone noticing. She smacked her palm against the metal hull. "Hey, anyone home?"

A man wearing a sealskin hat peered over the gunwale —Walton, if she remembered correctly. "Hi," she called, giving him her biggest grin and cutting the motor. "Is Captain Sobol on board?"

He pulled back without a word, replaced a moment later by another man with a dark beard and deep hazel eyes. The music went silent. "I'm Elias's first mate, Jacob. I'm afraid he isn't here."

Her heart sank, and heat rose to her face. Had Elias told them to give her the brush off? She reached for the painter line, readying her arm to toss it up to Jacob. "I really need to talk to him. Permission to come aboard."

He shook his head, eyes cold. "He's really not here, sweetheart."

She grit her teeth at being called sweetheart, but this guy was the gatekeeper at the moment, and she'd play nice if she had to. She tossed him the painter line, hearing it thud against the deck. He made no move to pick it up.

"Is he avoiding me?" she asked.

Three other men appeared at the gunwale. Now four sets of eyes glared at her. What had Elias told them? The zodiac drifted farther away, playing out the line between the two boats.

"Please," she begged them. "I need to apologize to him."

Jacob raised one eyebrow. "You do?"

She nodded, looking from one face to another. "Please tell him to come talk to me."

Jacob ran one big hand over the top of his hair, seeming to consider. "We haven't seen him since he called in your location. He handed the boat over to me. Said he was done with human life for a while."

Her heart threatened to beat its way out of her chest. "Done with human life? What does that mean?"

Running both hands down the silver sealskin covering his chest and shoulders, Jacob remained silent.

Elias is in seal form. Somehow, she knew that's what he meant. Her gaze shifted to the surrounding water, hoping to see Elias there. "For how long?"

The painter line slithered free of the *Utkin's* gunwale, falling into the water with a *plop*. Several yards of space now separated the boats. Jacob shrugged. "Could be days, could be decades. All I can say is that he's not here."

She started to reel in the loose line, eyes burning with unshed tears. How was she supposed to wait for decades? "Is there any way to reach him?"

The men glanced between themselves as if holding a conversation with only their eyes. She frowned, sure she could hear whispered voices, though their lips never moved. Finally, Jacob turned back to face her. "He's out of range, but if we do come into contact, I'll try to convince him to come talk to you."

She met his eyes, chest aching and hollow. She supposed this was no less than she deserved. "Thank you."

Turning the zodiac around, she headed back to the *Willy Nilly* to set about fixing her frayed wiring. If she wanted to keep her boat, she had fish to catch. But her mind kept returning to the one that had gotten away.

CHAPTER SEVENTEEN

*D*ays passed with no sign of Elias. Lana's anxiety grew, and she found herself looking for seals more often than salmon as the weeks wore on. Joe had returned to his family in Dillingham after the accident, leaving Lana and Jeanette to man the boat by themselves. Lana knew she ought to hire a replacement, but it felt too exhausting to interview people for the position, so she let it slide. Today was closed to commercial fishing, and Jeanette had the day off.

There was plenty to do on the boat, but Lana didn't want to be alone. Leaving the *Willy Nilly* at anchor, she headed to the bakery to visit with Ashlyn. She used the back door, tying one of the aprons around her waist as she entered the kitchen.

Ashlyn was cutting cinnamon rolls, and Kepler sat on a stool drinking coffee, the lapels of his dark suit dusted with crumbs.

"You're looking spiffy today," Lana said. "Where've you been?"

"Had to testify at a trial in Anchorage." Kepler grinned at her, eyes twinkling. "Ashlyn was just telling me you're one of us now."

Lana brushed the crumbs off the front of his suit jacket. Kepler had become like the brother she never had. "Sort of. I haven't seen him since the island. And I haven't been to the glacier for my spirit animal."

"Still a no-show, huh?" Kepler narrowed his eyes. "He can't claim you and disappear like some deadbeat mate. I'm going to track him down and have a few words."

Lana usually would have been grateful for help speeding things up, but she didn't think Elias would respond well to that kind of confrontation. "Please don't. I'm the deadbeat mate in this situation."

Kepler let out a slow breath and pulled her into a hug. She she couldn't hold back a sob, and he patted her back. "He's your mate. He'll come around. Give him time."

"I'm terrible at waiting." She sniffled.

Ashlyn brought her a cup of coffee and pointed to the counter where a dark bottle of Baileys sat. "There's some morning fortitude, if you want."

Lana didn't usually imbibe so early in the day, but she needed all the fortification she could get right now. She added a heavy dose of the liqueur and took a sip, the slightly sweet creaminess filling her mouth with pleasant warmth. "All right, enough about me. What can I do to help?"

She was rolling out sugar cookie dough when Cal popped in, greeting her with his usual flippant, "Hey," before heading straight for the tray of bear claws.

"Cal!" Ashlyn swept the tray away before he could snag a second pastry. "Unless you're going to pay for those, hands off."

He gave her a sheepish grin then turned to frown at Lana. "Still no sign of him?"

Lana shook her head. Was this going to be the primary topic of conversation for the rest of her life? "I scared him off pretty good, I guess."

"*You* scared *him* off?" Cal snorted. "He's supposed to be the scary monster, not you. Is he a selkie or a pussy?"

Ashlyn hit him in the shoulder hard enough to make him wince. "Your mouth is going to get you a bloody nose, Cal."

"What?" He took a bite of pastry and glared at his Alpha. "I'm only saying I assumed it would be the other way around."

Tears blurred Lana's eyes, and she had to turn away. She stared at the animal-shaped cookie cutters. She'd called Elias a monster right before she said she hated him.

"I don't understand how his crew can't find him. Where would he go?" Kepler asked.

"I assume he's out there swimming around in seal form somewhere." Her hand froze on the orca-shaped cookie cutter. "Oh, God, what if something happened to him? What if a killer whale ate him or something?"

"You have a special bond, Lana," Ashlyn said. "You'd know if he died."

"Oh." She pressed the cutter into the dough. "How long can shifters stay in animal form?"

"I'm not sure. A long time, I guess," Kepler said. "But most people prefer the comforts available to humans."

Cal swiped another bear claw while Ashlyn's back was turned. "I had an aunt who ran with a bunch of regular wolves up in Denali for eight solid years. But she always was a little loony."

Ashlyn pulled the cinnamon rolls from the proofing rack and transferred them to the oven. "Even regular seals have to rest on land sometimes, right? Maybe you could check out beaches where seals hang out."

Lana froze, staring sightlessly at the wall across from her. She pictured Elias pulling himself onto the beach, transforming into the glorious man that he was. "Not beaches. The beach. *Our* beach." If Elias would go on land anywhere, it would be their beach. The place they'd bonded. She turned, ripping off her apron. "I have to go."

"Pretty sure you can't get to that beach by boat," Cal said.

"Jesus, Cal," Ashlyn said, punching him again. "Show a little support."

He scowled at her and straightened his uniform. "It's not like I can help. The chopper's for official use only."

Lana said, "A big boat can't get there, but I could anchor it and take the zodiac in. Except what am I going to tell Jeanette?"

"Do you have to take her?" Kepler asked. "Maybe someone on the *Utkin* will help you. I'm sure they want their Alpha back as much as you do."

Ashlyn grabbed a pink box of doughnuts and thrust it at her. "Here. Bribes always help."

"Thanks." Lana gave her cousin and Kepler quick hugs and nodded at Cal.

He winked back. "Good luck."

At the river, she guided the zodiac toward the *Utkin*, surprised to find Jacob there waiting. "Hey, Lana."

Her already racing heart sped up until she could hardly breathe. "Is he back?"

Jacob shook his head. "Nope."

Bobby appeared at Jacob's side, then Jeanette peered shyly over the rail. Lana cocked an eyebrow. In the weeks since her return, she and Jeanette had grown quite fond of the *Utkin's* crew, and Jeanette had taken a shine to the tall, bearded deckhand. She thought about warning her friend off, but then remembered Elias saying that most shifters never found their mates. Who was she to interfere?

She reached for the pastry box. "Brought these for you guys. Watch out, though, or Jeanette will eat all the maple bars."

Bobby guffawed. "Is that where they all went last time?"

Jeanette flushed scarlet. "It was the only food on board."

"Jeanette," Lana interrupted, "I hate to ask, but I need you back on the *Willy Nilly*." She'd decided if she was going to ask Elias's crew for help, it would be best to have them drop her off. And she had to leave someone behind to watch the *Willy Nilly* in case she was gone a while. "And I need to talk to you, Jacob. In private."

"Of course." Jeanette climbed down the side and they swapped out positions on the zodiac.

As Jeanette puttered away, Lana turned to Jacob. The other men stood around looking at her curiously. "I want you to take me back to the island."

He cocked his head. "You think he's there?"

"He's got to rest on land sometimes, right? He'll be there. I just know it."

Jacob turned to his crew mates, and after what seemed to be a silent debate, he shrugged. "Okay. Guess it's worth a shot."

CHAPTER EIGHTEEN

*E*lias pulled up on the shore, transforming to his human self before sitting to stare out at the water. He felt as if he'd left his heart on this beach, buried like stolen treasure, never to be found. Sitting next to the remains of the fire pit, he sifted sand through his fingers. Lana had touched this very sand. Sat in this very spot. Made love with him under this very sky. Those few days with Lana had been the highlight of his life. Now he'd never know those moments again.

"I shouldn't be here," he said to a gull drifting overhead. Since Lana had rejected him, he'd spent all his days in seal form, drifting with the current and living off the ocean's bounty. But being in seal form so long was taking its toll on him. He was tired. His legs felt wobbly, and his fingertips clumsy in the gritty sand.

The sun beating down on his human skin made it tighten uncomfortably.

The sound of a small boat motor echoed off the water. Someone was nearby. They weren't likely to approach too closely due to the submerged rocks, but he didn't want to be spotted. This place was his and Lana's, and he wanted to keep it that way.

Rising, he took one step toward the water, intending to return to the sea, then changed his mind. He was too tired, and longed to nap under the boughs of the spruce tree that held so many memories. *Our tree.* He turned and hiked inland to the spot. The low branches scratched his skin as he crawled beneath them, fingers digging into the thick carpet of moss and needles. He could swear the air here still smelled faintly of Lana, and his chest ached with longing.

Under the dappled light, he spotted the heart she had carved into the trunk, back when he'd believed she might possibly love him. The wound oozed sap, beads trailing down the bark as if the carving bled.

"Fitting," he muttered.

He frowned and moved closer to the carving, staring at the pale slashes in the gray bark. L plus E had been carved inside the heart. Who had added that? He reached out and traced it, fingers getting tacky from the sap. *Lana?* But when?

The sound of the boat grew louder. His heart beat faster. Why would someone come here? *They're looking for you.* He'd felt the presence of his crew brush his mind a few times since he'd left them, but he always shut them out, diving to the bottom of the sea until the sensation passed.

This presence felt different. More urgent.

Over the sound of the waves, he heard a hull scrape sand. Then footsteps. The ever present breeze wafted a familiar scent in his direction, cinnamon and mocha. A name left his mouth, his voice creaking from disuse. "Lana?"

The boughs at the entrance parted, and her lovely face peered in at him. But instead of smiling, like in his dreams, her features crumpled into tears. She choked out, "You're here."

Tears. What was he supposed to do with tears? Did she still hate him? His seal didn't care. His mate was in pain. Before he could stop himself, he reached out and pulled her to him, settling her onto his lap under the branches.

She clung to him like a life preserver, burying her face against his neck and peppering his bare skin with kisses and tears.

His muscles refused to move. His brain refused to work. Was he dreaming? This had to be a dream, like all the dreams he'd had of her while she was married to Peter. She hated him.

"I'm sorry I called you a monster," she said.

He shook his head. "No, you were right. I acted like a monster. I should never have kept you on this island. I should've gone for help right away."

"You saved my life, and I treated you like crap. I acted like a child. I don't hate you. Exactly the opposite, in fact."

He drew in a deep breath, filling his lungs with her scent as his arms tightened around her. Had she just said what he thought she'd said? "What is the opposite?"

She pulled back a fraction, sniffling. "I want you in my life."

Not love, then. Just the power of fate insisting they be together. "I want to be near you, too, Lana. To bring you joy. But all I do is disappoint you. I make you angry."

"No!" She squeezed him back. "Ashlyn says this up and down feeling is normal at first. It will level out the longer we're together." She tilted her head and looked into his eyes, hers reddened by tears. "I just... After Peter, I have issues with marriage."

A growl rose in his throat at the mention of her late husband. "You still love him."

Her eyes widened. "What? Why would you think that?"

"He's all you ever talk about."

She shook her head. "I love *you*, Elias. I didn't know what love was until I met you. Peter cheated on me, accused me of things I didn't do, made me feel small. He made me afraid of love." Her voice grew softer, more hesitant. "You make me feel worthy."

He stared at her for a long moment. "You are the most worthy woman I've ever met. I never understood why a smart, strong woman like you would put up with a man like that. I was waiting for you to leave him."

"I thought if I just tried harder, I could make it work. But it never did."

Elias stroked one palm down the back of her soft hair. Gods, he'd missed her. "I love you, Lana. With every ounce of my being. I will worship you forever, whether we marry or not."

She put her fingertips against his cheek, stroking the beard that had grown longer during his time away. In a husky voice, she said, "I want to be with you."

Without a second thought, he rolled her off his lap and onto the cushion of needles. He lowered his mouth to hers, crushing her lips in a hungry kiss. She responded by opening wide, her tongue darting against his as she adjusted her hips to settle him between her thighs. Already hard, he ground against her center, eliciting a moan.

She reached for the waist of her jeans, getting them open and unzipped while he pushed her shirt up over her breasts, kneading the soft mounds of flesh through her bra. Her nipples tightened beneath the fabric, and he growled in frustration at the thin barrier between her skin and his. Rearing back onto his knees, he pulled off his pelt and tossed it aside, then stripped her pants and shirt from her until she lay naked below him. Between the branches, sunlight dappled her pale skin, pink nipples, and the dusky curls between her legs.

He dropped to his elbows and buried his face in her scent, mouthing over her lower lips while his hands curled around her ass and squeezed. She bucked up against him, and he lifted her legs, dipping his tongue into her well of sweetness again and again until she writhed.

"Heaven," he breathed against her, then slipped a finger inside. Her heat enveloped him, her slickness coating his fingers as her inner walls tightened in response. He added a second finger, then a third, rubbing slowly in and out.

"Elias, oh, yes!"

He sucked her clit, circling the nub with his tongue. She exploded around him, crying out and arching her back, muscles pulsing rhythmically.

His cock throbbed with need, and as soon as she relaxed, he covered her, looking into her flushed face with adoration. Her pupils were dilated, her breath in panting gasps. "Take me," she begged.

"Tell me you're mine." He pressed the head of his shaft between her folds, teasing the entrance. Lana flexed her hips upward, striving for more, but he held back. "Mine," he repeated.

"I'm yours, Elias. And you're mine."

He thrust forward in one sure stroke, filling her, becoming one with her. She whimpered and spread her legs, her inner walls fluttering again. Wanting to drive her higher, he pulled back and thrust forward again, hips hard against her soft flesh. In and out he stroked, building her passion. A scream rose from her throat and her nails dug into him as she reached the crest. He pistoned harder, his own climax nearing its peak. He released inside her in a rush of heat, stars filling his vision. A tide of pleasure swept him under, and he wasn't sure he could ever emerge.

As he became aware of his surroundings again, he felt the pressure of her blunt teeth against his shoulder. Her gentle bite didn't break skin, but it turned him on all over again. "What are you doing?" he growled against her ear, pumping between her legs a few more times.

"Claiming you." She nipped him again. "You're mine."

He chuckled. "My ferocious little mate."

They snuggled there under his pelt in contentment for a long time before he finally asked, "How did you get here?"

"Your crew dropped me off. I borrowed the skiff."

He pulled her back against his chest and drew his knees up until his body cocooned hers. He never wanted to leave this moment, but he'd been gone from his crew too long. "I suppose we should head back."

"Jacob can handle things." She twisted to face him, a naughty gleam in her eyes. "I'm going to keep you trapped on this island just a little while longer."

Grinning, he nibbled her tender earlobe. "I'm happy to be your captive."

EPILOGUE

*L*ana took another sip of her beer and laughed as Dean reenacted wrestling with an octopus that had been caught in his net. The big dining room in the house Elias shared with his crew had been rearranged with two more tables to accommodate the crowd celebrating Lana's final payment on the *Willy Nilly*. This had been a bumper season, and Lana had the feeling Elias's crew had been surreptitiously driving schools of salmon into her net.

Both crews, plus Ashlyn and her pack, had just polished off the biggest pan of paella Lana had ever seen. Elias had turned out true to his word about cooking, and Lana was glad fishing burned so many calories, or she wouldn't fit into her clothes any more. She might have to join a gym over the winter to keep the pounds off.

Dean flailed his arms in front of him wildly. "The octopus kept sliding its tentacles into my pants. I couldn't keep up with all those arms."

"She was fishing for a minnow," Jacob joked.

Dean gave him a dirty look. "Very funny. Those suckers leave welts, you know."

"Leave it to Dean to attract an octopus mate," Walton slurred. He was a lightweight when it came to beer.

An awkward silence swept the room as everyone avoided glancing toward Jeanette. She was the only one here who didn't know about shifters, and sometimes things slipped. But the way Bobby had his arm draped across the back of the small woman's chair and kept toying with the ends of Jeanette's hair made Lana wonder how much longer her crew mate would be left in the dark.

Thankfully, Bobby changed the subject. "How about some music?"

Everyone clapped in approval, and while he went to retrieve his fiddle, Ashlyn started clearing dishes. Lana rose. "Sit, I'll do it."

"I'm pregnant, not crippled," Ashlyn said, continuing to clear plates.

"I'm just saying you're our guest, you shouldn't work." Lana shook her head, but didn't stop her cousin from lending a hand. Ashlyn had announced the news a few weeks ago, and now all the men treated her like a China doll.

Jeanette joined them, carrying an armload of dishes into the kitchen. "I've never had paella before. It was delicious. Everything Bobby prepares makes my mouth catch fire. You're lucky to have a boyfriend who can cook." She shook her head. "Although I'm still flabbergasted about how you went from hating to dating."

Lana shrugged and started loading plates into the dishwasher. "I guess I'm a sucker for a knight in shining armor."

"Well, I'm glad. I like his crew." Jeanette flushed. "And Elias is nice, too. You think he'll ask you to marry him?"

"We've discussed it," Lana said, pulling another beer from the fridge. "If we ever have kids, I might consider it." She'd been thinking about marriage a lot since Ashlyn had revealed her pregnancy. All the things Lana wanted to avoid by not getting married were already coming true. Her friends were Elias's friends. When she wasn't here at his house, he was at hers. He was there to lend a hand with her boat. Sure, he could come off as a little bossy, but when she disagreed with him, he let her go her own way. And not once since the island had he pressured her about getting married again.

Ashlyn shot her a pleased glance, but didn't comment. Her cousin knew it was a touchy subject. As a Cajun tune rolled in from the other room, Ashlyn opened a pastry box, revealing cupcakes decorated with spikes of yellow, orange, and red frosting. "I made these especially for tonight."

"Fire?" Lana raised her eyebrows. "What does that have to do with fishing?"

"Do you ever think about anything but fish?" Ashlyn laughed. "It's a mortgage burning. Usually people do it when they pay off their home, but I thought it fit since you spend more time on that boat than you do in your house."

Lana beamed. "You know me so well."

They carried the cupcakes to the dining room and handed them out. Cal swiped two, and Dean complained until Ashlyn offered him a second one. "I know this crowd, so I made plenty. There are more in the kitchen."

Licking frosting from her fingers, Lana scooted her chair close to Elias, sitting hip-to-hip with him. He put his arm around her, letting her lean against his chest. They listened to a few more songs, and she basked in the camaraderie filling the room. These people were her people, her family, her clan. She'd lived so isolated when she was married to Peter, she'd forgotten how having close friendships could feel. Elias had given her all of this. And because of him, she was going to get even more.

A spirit animal.

Tomorrow he would take her to the glacier. If they didn't have guests tonight, she'd already have him on the road. She hated waiting. It gave her too much time to think. She tilted her face to look up at Elias and whispered, "Walton was kidding about octopus shifters, right?"

He gave her a reassuring squeeze. "I'm fairly certain only warm-blooded creatures can be spirit animals."

That gave her enough relief to settle back and enjoy the night. As Bobby wrapped up a final song, Elias held his drink high in the air. "A toast to Lana's success. May we always look forward with pleasure, never backward with regret."

Everyone raised their bottles in the air and cheered. It was the perfect toast. The perfect night. Lana grinned at him. "How did I never recognize you are so wonderful?"

He cocked an eyebrow. "Too busy hating me, I guess."

She smiled, knowing he was right. Trust and love for him swelled inside her chest until it hurt. He'd made her into a stronger woman. Her past had been dark and suppressed, but here, in this moment, her past didn't matter. Elias was her only, fated, true mate.

In this moment, all she saw was her future.

*L*ana stood facing the wall of ice, and although it was only late September, she wrapped her arms around herself against the frigid air. An enormous harvest moon hung low in the inky sky, casting pale light over the glacier that had been strikingly blue under the setting sun. At their feet, a thin layer of ice covered a vast lake. She only knew this because Elias had stepped too close to the edge and broken through.

He poured water from his boot and put it back on, impervious to the bone-chilling water. "I can't wait until you get your seal and we can swim in this."

"As long as I don't fall in before I get my animal." She shook off the sudden image of herself as a scruffy marmot diving beneath the ice. The possibility she might not get a seal for an animal—or a sea animal at all—weighed heavily on her.

This was their second night waiting for the Source to reveal itself; according to shifter lore, the cave would find them, not the other way around, but Lana was not happy just sitting around and waiting. She looped her arm through Elias's. "Let's keep looking."

"You're so impatient," he said, his voice full of affection.

"Walking keeps me warm." She stopped in front of a sign warning them not to proceed without a guide and looked at the steep path ahead. So far, they'd stuck to the area marked with orange cones by the park experts. "I think we need to move off the trail. The cave might not show itself where other people might see it."

Ashlyn had been dropped by helicopter on the ice, and the cave had opened up a short distance away, easy peasy. Lana envied her cousin's experience as the cold wind wormed its way between her layers of clothing. How many nights would she have to spend out here?

She started up an incline between two walls of ice, putting her gloved hand against one side to help her balance. The wall cut off her view of the moon, plunging her into darkness. She tapped her foot along the ice to be certain of her next step.

The ice shuddered under her feet and she froze, terrified. What if a crevasse opened and swallowed her and Elias? She could fall to her death before any magic even happened. *There's a reason the park maintains trails.* Both palms flat against the ice wall beside her, she turned around. "Let's go back."

Elias met her gaze, eyes glowing slightly with silver light. "It's here."

"What?"

He pointed past her. "Keep going."

She turned. Faint blue light shone from a crack in the wall ahead. "Oh my God."

Scrambling up the slope, she reached a narrow opening. The moment she stepped inside, blue light crackled through the ice, illuminating an enormous cavern. She gasped, groping behind her for Elias's hand.

He stepped up beside her, putting one arm around her shoulder and pulling her close as they both took a moment to look around.

Walls and ceiling glistening glacier blue, the space was the size of a football stadium with a glowing blue floor dotted with dark stones and gravel. Several yards from where Lana stood, a flat boulder created what looked like a raft in the glowing ice, and a trickle of water flowed in a steady stream directly onto it from the ceiling, filling the cave with a soft pattering sound.

"The Source," Elias breathed reverently. "I never imagined I'd see it myself."

Lana took a step forward but halted as the blue light exploded into a rainbow of colors, dancing across the ceiling in ribbons and bursts. She realized her mouth was hanging open, and her chest felt tight against her fluttering breath. "It's gorgeous."

Sweat prickled over her skin beneath her parka, and lowered her zipper, letting in a cool wash of air. Elias wrapped both arms around her from behind and rested his chin on top of her head. He felt solid and warm at her back, and his voice rumbled through her pleasantly. "I feel so blessed."

Turning, she lifted her face to his and kissed him. "Promise you'll still feel that way if I end up as a seagull?"

"Worry wart." He nipped her nose. "Now get naked."

She cocked an eyebrow. "All you think about is sex."

"I do. But I also thought you'd prefer not to ruin your clothes when you shift."

"Oh, excellent point." She shrugged out of her parka and gloves, handing them to Elias. The air was still chilly, but not like it had been outside the cave.

Taking a deep breath, she approached the Source slowly, her skin tingling the closer she got. Most shifters had never seen this place, the origin of their power; they didn't need to unless they ended up taking a human mate. Ashlyn had said she'd approached through a tunnel and had never mentioned the vast pool filling the back half of the cavern. Smooth as glass, the water reflected the dancing light from the ceiling, and Lana swore she caught a whiff of ocean air.

Encouraged, she stripped out of the rest of her clothing until she stood barefoot on the rocky floor at the edge of the boulder. The rough, uneven edges against her bare feet reminded her of the island, the place that had changed her life forever. Now this place was about to do the same.

Heartbeat thudding in her ears, she stepped up onto the flat boulder. The water dripping from the ceiling coated the stone and slicked a path down toward the edge of the pool.

Stepping up right next to the stream, she cupped her hands beneath it, filling her palms with the cold liquid. Her mouth felt dry, as if encouraging her to drink. Lowering her mouth, she slurped from her hands, taking long swallows as the stream replenished the water. It was crisp and refreshing, exactly how she'd imagine glacier water would taste, but it settled into the pit of her stomach with surprising warmth.

She stopped drinking and dropped her hands, looking down at her naked belly as the heat inside her grew. It felt like it was burning a trail through her veins, leading to her shoulders and hips. *Did I drink too much? God, what if it's poison?* Sudden panic gripped her, and she turned to face Elias. "I'm scared."

Only her words didn't come out as words. They emerged as a strange sort of hoot. What the fuck? *Please don't let me be a bird.* She squeezed her eyes shut, her body refusing to hold her upright any longer. Her knees and palms hit the hard stone, and her stomach heaved as if trying to wretch up the water.

Slowly, the heat subsided, and her rapid breathing eased. She cracked open her eyes to find herself still in the cavern, lying with her cheek against the stone. The desire to go swimming filled her, a desire that wasn't entirely her own.

She lifted her head and twisted to look down at her body. Silver fur with dark spots covered her sleek torso that tapered to a short pair of flippers. *Seal?*

A joyful presence filled her, a voice that was and yet wasn't her own. And she knew. *I'm a seal!* Ecstatic, she searched the cave for Elias, calling out in that cooing squeak again.

In her head, she heard her lover's voice. *Come play with me.*

She knew he and his crew could communicate through thought, but had not experienced it until now. The feeling was odd, but comforting. *Where are you?*

The water is amazing! At the edge of the pool, a pile of clothing lay on the rocks, and a ring of concentric circles rippled over the pool's surface.

She slid off the boulder, clumsy in this new form, and hitched herself toward the water. The moment she slipped below the surface, her muscles took over as if she'd been in this form all her life. She torpedoed through as if she was flying. The dancing lights no longer seemed to be coming from the ceiling but flowed all around her in waves, making her feel as if she was swimming among the stars.

Elias's darker form was easy to spot, and she headed toward him, circling and dancing in a water ballet for two. Her heart raced, and she picked up speed, heading for the surface. She breached and jackknifed her body to re-enter the water in a smooth plunge, spiraling downward. Her seal was singing, releasing bubbles as she descended, sharing her joy. It was as if a part of her had been missing her entire life, and she'd never realized it until now.

She swam until her muscles burned and her lungs ached. Surfacing next to Elias, she yawned. *I never imagined it could be like this.*

You are beautiful, he replied, and although his seal face couldn't exactly smile, she felt him beaming through their connection.

Can your crew hear us?

No, they're too far away. And this feels different from when I speak with them. Clearer. I think our mate bond strengthens it.

She leaned back, floating lazily as she looked up toward the ceiling. Her seal was telling her it was time to go, but she hated to leave. *I wish this pool had fish in it. I'm hungry.*

Elias nudged her toward shore, pushing her like a raft. She let him, loving the lap of the water over her pelt. It felt surprisingly warm. When her back scraped ice and stone, she turned and clambered awkwardly onto the beach. Elias transformed with ease, laying his pelt out over the rocks and ice like a beach blanket.

Lana stared, trying to figure out how to shift back. Her seal didn't want to relinquish control. *How do I become human again?*

"Giving you pushback, is she?" Elias said out loud as he sat on his pelt with his legs outstretched. She still had a hard time believing this gorgeous man wanted to be with a frumpy fisherwoman like her. He leaned back on his hands as if preparing to watch a show. "Think about your knees—that's how my dad taught me. It'll help you get in touch with your human body, since seals don't have knees."

She closed her eyes and imagined bending her knees. All she could think about was skinning them when she was a kid. She was imagining the slight pain of the cuts when she heard Elias say, "Good job!"

Opening her eyes, she realized she was on her hands and knees against the gravel and ice. "Huh," she huffed and stood. Something heavy and wet lay over her shoulders. *My pelt.* She ran her hands along the fur. It was softer than Elias's, and quite lovely under the glimmering lights. She wrinkled her nose, realizing that from now on, she would need to wear the sealskin, no matter the season.

"What do I do with this, now?" she asked. "Can I make it smaller?"

Elias shrugged, pulling his human clothing back on. "You control it by imagining what you want it to become, like how you thought about your knees to transform. If you prefer something small, you could make it into a hat like Walton's."

"That's fine for winter, but Walton looks like a dork wearing it all summer. What about earrings? Could I make it that small?" She thought hard about squeezing the fur down into the size of earrings. To her surprise, the fur responded, shrinking and dividing. She cupped her hands over her ears, and the fur centered there.

Elias burst into a laugh. "You're lopsided."

She wrinkled her nose at him and leaned over the pool, finding her reflection staring back at her with two huge puffs of fur that looked more like earmuffs than earrings. One was the size of a softball while the other was more petite, fitting over her ear sleekly.

"That was actually impressive, especially for your first try." Elias came up behind her, his reflection grinning at her. "But separating your pelt into pairs is hard. That's why you'll hardly ever find a selkie wearing sealskin boots."

"But not impossible, right?" Lana said, pressing against the larger earmuff until she was happier with its size. It still didn't match completely, but it would do for now. And she promised herself she would figure out how to make earrings, eventually.

She turned to model them for Elias. "Better?"

He scanned her naked body. "Perfect."

"You're not even looking at my pelt!"

He stepped close and ran his hands down her bare sides, then back up to cup her breasts. Her nipples responded immediately, hardening under his touch and tingling with the need for more. He leaned in and claimed her mouth, his lips soft but demanding. She wrapped both arms around his neck and kissed him back. The heat between them grew, and the ice shuddered under their feet.

Elias broke the kiss and glanced toward the ceiling. The lights were weaker, the ice paler, as if the sun glowed through from outside. "I think the spirits are telling us it's time to go."

She nodded. Her seal was telling her that, as well. But she was also feeling a small bit of panic, as if she was about to lose something precious. She needed him to know how much she loved him. To declare it now, under these lights, for all the spirits to see. To tell the universe that they were meant to be together. He bent to pick up her clothes, and she grabbed his hand. "Elias."

He turned back to her, a slight frown knitting his eyebrows. "Yes?"

"Marry me."

His hand tightened around hers. "Are you sure?"

She swallowed, the impulse inside her too strong to resist, especially with her seal wanting it, too. "Yes. Let's do it."

His face broke into a grin, and he nodded. "I love you, Lana."

"I love you, too." Enough to tie herself to him forever in every way possible.

She dressed, and they headed for the cave entrance. Daylight painted the ice wall opposite the opening in creamy orange light. Lana took one last glance over her shoulder at the cave. The aurora inside flashed, as if saying goodbye, and then subsided back to an aquamarine glow. When they stepped outside, the opening shuddered closed.

This was just the beginning for her and her mate. Her life was starting anew, and she no longer had to face it alone.

Together, she and Elias walked off the glacier and into the light of a new day.

Dear Reader,

I hope you enjoyed this surly selkie and his reluctant mate! My next Alaska Alpha takes us back to land, with a pregnant heroine on the run.

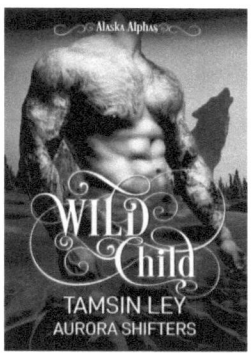

When a huge, tat-covered bounty hunter tracks Melody down, she knows she's out of options. Yet something about him makes her insides quiver with something besides fear...

Order your copy of Wild Child now or keep reading for a sneak peek. Thank you for reading!

Love, Tamsin

P.S. Be sure to check out all the Alaska Alphas books at https://books2read.com/rl/AuroraShifters

WILD CHILD EXCERPT

*A*sh pulled his ski hat down over his forehead to block the bitter wind coming in off the inlet. Downtown Anchorage in February could feel like the North Pole, despite the sun hitting the dirty snow lining the street. Even his inner wolf was curled up in a ball, content to avoid being called on to do anything in this frigid weather. Pink sidewalk salt crunched under Ash's boots as he skirted a cart selling reindeer sausage. The Fur Rendezvous festival was gearing up, and despite the temperature, the sidewalks teemed with people.

He'd gotten word that the heiress he was tracking had been selling of her jewelry at a pawn shop nearby, and the bounty on her was big—twenty-five thousand plus expenses. The reward would be enough to make a sizable dent in what he owed the pack. But only if he caught up to her before the other bounty hunters.

He waited for traffic to pass so he could cross the street, listening to the music from the carnival a few blocks down. Ahead, the wrought iron bars over the pawn shop windows glittered with frost, reminiscent of the cheap bling Ash knew was inside. The equally frosty glass obscured a mishmash of objects displayed for sale inside. A familiar, wiry figure stepped out of the shop, looked both directions, then locked eyes with Ash. *Damn it.* Talvin, a fox shifter from Bootlegger's Cove. Usually, he made his living serving papers for one of the local attorneys, but had also been known to pull in a bounty or two.

Ash darted across the street in front of a Suburban, ignoring the angry horn blast. He had to find out what Talvin had discovered before the man disappeared into the crowd. Skidding to a stop on the sidewalk, Ash planted one hand against the side of the building to stop Talvin from rounding the corner.

Talvin cringed, zipping his worn coat up to his throat. "Hey, Ash. What's up?"

The guy knew why he was here, and Ash was in no mood for small talk. "What'd you find out?"

"Hey, I'm just shopping." The smaller man took a step back. "I don't want no trouble."

Ash ran his tongue along his front teeth and forced himself to calm down, conscious of a woman in a bulky parka covered with Fur Rendezvous pins passing behind him on the sidewalk. The last thing he needed was for someone to call the police. He was on APD's shit list, and they'd haul him in and ask questions later. Then he'd lose this bounty for sure.

Making his voice as calm as possible, he asked, "What'd you buy?"

Talvin pulled a phone out of his pocket. "New phone, man. Can I go?"

Chest tight, Ash lowered his arm, calling on his wolf's senses to take in the other shifter's scent as Talvin darted away. If he needed to, he could track the fox down after talking to the clerk inside the store. He waited until Talvin disappeared around the corner before pushing open the pawn shop door.

A door chime played an off-key rendition of Jingle Bells as he stepped into the scent of dust and old machine grease. He allowed his eyes a moment to adjust to the dim interior, noting the old theater curtain masking the back portion of the store as he tucked his gloves into his pocket. In the main area, odds and ends stacked the walls from ceiling to floor, everything from used bicycles and camping gear to toys and even a beat-up mannequin in a lavishly beaded wedding gown. Immediately to his left, a balding clerk with glasses sat on a stool between two glass-topped counters packed with guns and jewelry.

The man laid a tattered Louis L'Amour paperback face down on the counter behind him and pushed his glasses up his nose. "Buying or selling?"

Ash pulled a picture from his pocket. The woman he was tracking was from a red wolf pack down south, a pretty girl with a rounded face, plump lips, and long brown hair. Exactly Ash's type, though he couldn't concern himself with that. She wasn't smiling at the camera, but there was a glint in her eye that told him there was more to her than just her pretty looks. He held the photo out. "I'm looking for this woman. She been around here lately?"

The guy looked up at the stained acoustic ceiling tiles with a sigh. "God damn it. You're the second guy tasing about her today. Is the stuff she's been selling me hot?"

"I wouldn't know," Ash said, pocketing the photo. *Should've known Talvin was lying.* He'd take care of that later. Right now, he needed to see what the clerk could tell him. "Her family hired me to find her. Any of the stuff she sold you still here?" If he could pick up a fresh scent, his wolf might be able to track her.

The clerk slid open the back of the glass counter and pulled out a diamond tennis bracelet. Even in the crappy florescent light, the diamonds glittered luxuriously. The piece had to be worth at least eight grand. "She brought this in last week. Not sure how I'm going to sell it, but I got it for a steal."

Ash reached for it, but the clerk pulled back, eying the tattoos on Ash's hand. "Look, no touch."

Staring the man down, Ash asked, "How am I supposed to judge if it's real?" It was, of course. The woman was an heiress, after all. But Ash wasn't interested in whether it was real or not. He just needed a good sniff.

The guy hesitated a moment as if considering, then slowly extended his arm. "All right. Just know I have a gun if you do anything funky."

"I don't doubt that you do." Ash nodded respectfully and took the bracelet, pretending to examine the gems as he inhaled. The clerk's scent was topmost, a lingering odor of ham sandwich and beer. But there was another fragrance underneath, something that reminded him of rich velvet and chocolate.

Ash's wolf perked up. *Mate.*

Stand down, buddy. It had been a long time since Ash had been with a woman, but mates were rare, and the scent was too faint to jump to a rash conclusion like that. *Once we bag this bounty, we'll go out and celebrate.*

Handing the bracelet back to the clerk, Ash asked, "Anyone else look at this recently?"

The man's face lit up. "You interested? I'll give you an excellent deal."

"No. I asked if anyone else had looked at this." Luxuries were the last thing on Ash's mind. He needed to finish this job and pay off his debt. "What about that guy who was in here before me?"

The clerk scowled and shoved the bracelet back into the case beside the other bits of jewelry displayed on a black velvet tray. "Like I told him, I'm not in the information business. If you're not interested in buying, please leave."

Sighing, Ash dug in his pocket for his wallet. He pulled out his last twenty and placed it on the counter. "All I wanna know is if you know where that girl lives and if that fellow who was in here before me looked at any of her stuff."

The clerk crossed his arms and eyed the twenty before giving Ash a meaningful look.

"That's all I have," Ash said truthfully. Other than the punchcard for a local deli, his wallet was empty. Then he added, "She's in danger," he added. People always wanted to protect a pretty girl.

Pushing his glasses up his nose, the man shrugged, then snaked his hand out and swept the twenty off the counter and into his pocket. "She told me she likes the Chinese place down the street. I think she also mentioned something about her condo being in walking distance."

"Thanks."

Ash headed out the door, his wolf pushing to get out and follow the woman's scent. There were only a couple of condo developments nearby; picking up her scent should be a cakewalk.

He was going to bag himself an heiress.

"No, no, no!" Melody bumped her car crookedly against the curb as the engine sputtered and died. The check engine light had been on for a week, but she didn't have the money to get it fixed. She stared at the gauges on the dash, the heater blowing tepid air at full blast against the frost-rimmed windshield. *Now what?*

Taking a deep breath, she turned the car off, waited a second, and tried to start it again. The blower resumed, but the engine refused to turn over. Closing her eyes, she fought back tears. A mere six months ago, she'd have called for a taxi and let AAA handle the rest. But she didn't even have insurance right now, let alone roadside assistance.

"Be strong, Melody. The condo is only a few blocks away," she told herself. Her food was definitely going to be cold by the time she got home.

The inside of the car smelled of sesame chicken—Chinese food was one of the few things that smelled good since getting pregnant. She'd lost her job as a barista after only a few days because the scent of coffee made her vomit, and she had to retreat to the bathroom every ten minutes. Every other place she'd applied wanted references, and she couldn't risk leaving a trail; Brennan, the pack Alpha, had connections and wouldn't rest until he found her.

Until she could find another job, she'd been forced to rely on pawning her jewelry to pay rent. The bracelet she'd sold last week should've fetched four times the price she'd gotten, but she was a terrible negotiator. She had no idea how she was going to last until the baby was born, let alone take care of it afterward.

Now her car was kaput. She had to come up with a plan, fast, or she'd be forced to go back to her pack with her proverbial tail between her legs. She could picture the scar on Brennan's upper lip curling in pleasure as he deliberated on how to punish her for running away.

Baby fluttered against her bladder, a new sensation over the last week, reminding her of another urgent need; she had to pee. "All right, all right, I'm going," she said, picking up the loops of the white plastic bag with her food.

She stepped out of the car onto the icy curb and zipped her parka over her gently swelling belly, though it did little against the icy wind. Her cheeks were already numb. Adjusting her scarf up around her throat, she dug in her purse for some change for the meter.

A passing man in a wool dress coat, said, "That's a handicapped spot, in case you didn't notice."

Her shoulders sagged. He was right. She closed her purse and turned away. "Guess that's one way to get a free tow."

That got her a look from two women in designer ski parkas, so she clamped her mouth closed. Mom used to berate her for thinking out loud, but she couldn't seem to stop herself. Not even after Brennan gave her a bloody lip for speaking her mind.

Putting her back to the wind, she began trudging down the sidewalk toward home. A local festival was in full swing, filling the air with carnival music and laughter, and pedestrians hunched inside their parkas as they hurried along the sidewalks.

She turned the corner toward her condo. It was in a crappy district, but hadn't required references, and it had a spectacular view of Mt. Susitna. The Sleeping Lady, as the locals called it, reminded her of a pregnant woman, a comrade she often sat and talked to while alone in her living room. And since her escape from the pack, she was alone a lot.

"Better alone than in bad company," she said toward her belly.

The street sloped downward toward the industrial section of town and a bustling parking lot full of carnival rides. The building superintendent didn't seem to think the sidewalk along the street was part of his jurisdiction, so the path wasn't salted. Melody's designer boots had no traction on the ice, and she had to grip the fence rail for balance as she moved toward the side doorway. One block down, near the flashing lights of the carnival, what appeared to be a small child in a green snowsuit sailed into the air, arms flailing.

Melody paused, gaping. "What's going on?"

The crowd cheered, and the child seemed to cartwheel upward again.

If she hadn't been so cold, she might've continued past her condo to check things out, but the wind was driving daggers into her exposed cheeks. She rounded the gate post and headed toward the building. Maybe she'd be able to see the activity from her window.

Fingers stiff, she fumbled in her pocket for her keys before noticing that someone had left the door ajar—again. "Oh no."

She stepped inside and pulled the door firmly closed behind her, glancing around for signs of an intruder. Last time, a homeless guy had fallen asleep in the elevator and she'd had to use the stairs. Her place was on the third floor, and right now, her feet were numb. She pushed the elevator button. "Please be empty."

Thankfully, it was. The jerky ride to her floor reminded her she had to pee, and she raced to her front door. Dropping her now-cold food on the arm of the sofa, she locked the door behind her, then stripped out of her parka as she beelined it across the tiny living area, through her bedroom, and into the bathroom.

"Gotta pee, gotta pee, gotta pee," she chanted as she hurried to get her pants down. She was so chilly, even the hard toilet seat felt warm against her skin. Blessed relief filled her as she emptied her bladder.

She was washing her hands when she heard a creak, like someone was moving around her bedroom. Turning off the water, she stood still and listened.

Another floorboard popped.

Every muscle in her body tensed. Although she'd been born to shifter parents, she didn't have a shifter form to protect herself. Grandfather said mom had given her weak genes. *I should call the police.* Except her phone was in her coat pocket near the front door.

Breathing hard, she looked for something to use as a weapon. The only item in reach was the toilet brush, so she grabbed it and peered into the murky twilight of her bedroom. The blinds were shut, but there was enough light to see the bedcovers were rumpled, just as she'd left them. The closet didn't have any doors for someone to hide behind. Maybe she'd imagined it. The building *was* old and creaky.

Heart thundering, she crept into the room. The top drawer of her dresser hung open. Had she left it that way? The last of her jewelry was in that drawer, her only hope of staying afloat until after the baby was born and she could land another job. She grew light-headed. What if he'd already been in here when she got home and she hadn't noticed? The thief could be escaping right now.

Still wielding the toilet brush, she rushed toward the drawer and peered inside. She'd never been one for folding clothes, and her panties and bras lay jumbled inside. She gingerly nudged the lingerie aside, looking for the silk pouch with her jewelry.

It wasn't there.

"Mother fucker," she said out loud, anger displacing her fear.

She pivoted to the door. If the thief was still in the house, she was going to at least get a description to help the police catch the crook. How dare someone break in here and touch her things? She burst out of her bedroom into the small living area and collided against something solid. Huge. *And living.*

A giant, tattooed man stood between her and the exit.

Get your copy of Wild Child and keep reading now!

MORE ALASKA ALPHAS

These books all stand alone and can be read in any order.
Enjoy!

Free origin story!

Alpha Origins

Out Now!

Untamed Instinct by Tamsin Ley

Twisted Shifter by Tiele St. Clare

Bewitched Shifter by Tamsin Ley

Polar Shift by Boone Brux

Midnight Storm by Boone Brux

Midnight Son by Tiele St. Clare

Midnight Heat by Tamsin Ley

Too Wild to Mate by Tielle St. Clare

Wild Child by Tamsin Ley

Untamed Instinct

Bewitched Shifter

Midnight Heat

Wild Child

POST-APOCALYPTIC SCIENCE FICTION WRITTEN AS TAM LINSEY

Botanicaust

The Reaping Room

Doomseeds

Amarantox

ABOUT THE AUTHOR

Once upon a time I thought I wanted to be a biomedical engineer, but experimenting on lab rats doesn't always lead to happy endings. Now I blend my nerdy infatuation of science with character-driven romance and guaranteed happily-ever-afters. My monsters always find their mates, with feisty heroines, tortured heroes, and all the steamy trouble they can handle. I promise my stories will never leave you hanging (although you may still crave more!)

When I'm not writing, I'll be in the garden or the kitchen, exploring Alaska with my husband, or preparing for the zombie apocalypse. I also love wine and hard apple cider, am mediocre at crochet, and have the cutest 12-pound bunny named Abigail.

Interested in more about me? Join my VIP Club and get free books, notices, and other cool stuff!

www.tamsinley.com

bookbub.com/authors/tamsin-ley

goodreads.com/TamsinLey

facebook.com/TamsinLey

amazon.com/author/tamsin

ABOUT AURORA SHIFTERS

Aurora Shifters is a collaboration of Alaskan authors who decided to put our own Arctic spin on hot paranormal shapeshifters.

Tielle St. Clare moved to Alaska when she was seven years old and believes romances should be hot and sexy with a great story and fun characters. Learn more about her at www.tiellestclare.blogspot.com

Tamsin Ley was born and raised in Alaska and writes steamy sci-fi with a pinch of pixie dust. Find out more about her at www.tamsinley.com

Boone Brux has lived all over the world, finally settling in the icy region of Alaska. No person or escapade is off limits when it comes to weaving real life experiences into her books. Learn more at www.boonebrux.com

Be sure to join the Alaska Alphas Facebook Group! www.facebook.com/groups/alaskaalphas/

facebook.com/AlaskaAlphas

bookbub.com/authors/aurora-shifters

amazon.com/author/aurorashifters